Children For Sale

Taken

Grounded

Children For Sale

Taken

Jasper Joshua West

Grounded

ISBN: 9798601900942

Taken

Grounded

Table of Contents

Taken

Grounded

Taken

Chapter One

Jamie squinted, running from his classroom, his eyes adjusting to the sunlight after hours indoors. Being released for recess was so liberating after sitting inside for lessons all morning. It was an unusually hot day in Massachusetts, and he could already feel sweat forming on his neck as he ran. He faintly heard young girls singing and giggling in the distance as he sprinted as fast as he could to the swings.

The swing set is a hot commodity during every recess– and if you are not one of the first kids to grab a swing, you're out of luck for the day. When Jamie finally reached the swings, he was disappointed to find that three kids had already claimed them for the duration of their break. He frowned and made his way over to his usual spot during recess.

When Jamie's parents first told him that he would be moving to a new school, he was excited. For weeks he had been fantasizing about how wonderful it was going to be, until he walked into the classroom and realized that he was not prepared at all. There was so much in the room that it was hard to take it all in; posters displaying 3D shapes and famous people, and stations set up all around the room. It was so much better than he could ever have imagined.

Snack time was way better than at his old school and he loved art class, but what Jamie was looking forward to the most, and was struggling with the most, was making new friends.

He got to the corner of the fence where he usually sat while waiting for a swing and he sat down. Leaning on the fence, though, he felt himself starting to fall. He caught himself and moved over, looking for the reason for having fallen only to discover that the fence had been cut. He felt a bee sting his neck and he moved to smack it off of him, but what he felt was not an insect. He tried to remove the object when the world went black and he fell to the ground.

Chapter Two

Sharon Giles sighed as her house phone rang, interrupting the folding of laundry. She answered the phone to hear a chatter of incoherence, followed by, "Hello, is this Mrs. Giles?" the familiar voice asked.

"Yes, speaking," Sharon replied, trying to place the voice.

"This is Mrs. Spalding at Jamie's school," she said. Mrs. Spalding was the principal. "I'm afraid there is an emergency and we need you to come right away."

Sharon was hyperventilating as tears pooled in her eyes "Is Jamie okay?" she shouted into the phone, fearing the worst.

"Jamie disappeared during recess and we cannot find him anywhere," the principal replied with pity in her voice. "We've already called the police."

Without another word, Sharon hung up the phone, grabbed her keys and jumped into her car. She quickly pulled out and headed for the school. As soon as she was capable of speaking coherently, she called her husband over the Bluetooth in her car, praying that he would answer while he was at work. Harry picked up on the third ring "Sharon? Is something wrong?" he answered in a worried tone. He knew she wouldn't bother him unless it was important.

Sharon frantically explained the phone call from the school and assured her husband that she was on her way to meet the police and the staff at the school.

"I'm leaving work right now," Harry said, brow furrowed. "I'll be at the school in 15 minutes."

Fifteen minutes later, Sharon arrived at the school at the same time as her husband and saw a multitude of police cars parked around the administration block. She met the lead detective, Detective Boyd, and answered his preliminary questions about her son. She felt the passing time weighing down on her as she answered as patiently as was possible: he is 9 years old; he was wearing a blue shirt and jeans; yes, he knows not to talk to strangers. She was still frantically checking the time slowly ticking by on her phone when Detective Boyd confirmed that Jamie had not been found within a 10-mile radius and that the investigation had been escalated.

Only minutes later a detective rushed towards the group, speaking the three golden words: "We found something."

Taken

Jasper Joshua West

Chapter Three

Jamie slowly opened his eyes to find himself in an unfamiliar vehicle, and automatically assumed that he was dreaming. Looking to his left, he saw a sign informing him that he was leaving town. Looking up ahead he found that neither his mom nor his dad was driving. To his surprise, he did not see his mom's curly blonde hair or his dad's short black hair from his vantage point behind the driver's seat as he was accustomed to seeing.

Distracted by a slight movement at the far-right of the backseat, like someone trying to move as surreptitiously as possible, he focused his attention on the stranger looking at him in surprise. The woman with long, straight black hair, dull brown eyes, a nose piercing, and wearing a black dress was not anyone he recognized. He quickly made the assumption that it might well be a friend of one or both of his parents.

The woman spoke to the driver in a language unfamiliar to Jamie in an accent he could not pinpoint the origin of. This directed Jamie's attention back to the driver, who he was able to see more clearly now that he had turned to respond to the woman. He had a mean face, stringy black hair, and beady eyes that were constantly scanning his surroundings. When he opened his mouth to respond, chipped yellow teeth were visible, and his breath stank of alcohol and tobacco. He replied in the same language, and the woman began undressing Jamie, confusing him and causing some apprehension for the first time.

At this point, Jamie realized that the drive wasn't a dream and that he was in real danger from these foreigners transporting him from the only town he'd ever known in his short life. He began to panic, saw the man and woman nodding simultaneously at one another with serious expressions, and he opened his mouth to scream. It was at this moment that he saw the woman produce a syringe filled with a clear liquid which she injected into the same place on his neck in which he had been poked on the playground.

He felt himself slip into darkness as he screamed.

Chapter Four

To anyone looking in from the outside, Harry seemed very calm about the situation with his son, considering detectives suspected more than just a child leaving of his own accord. Harry had always been the type to take care of others before himself, especially his wife. Harry was focused on making sure his wife was calm and trying to keep her from having a breakdown, despite his already having started. How could anyone dare to take his smart, wonderful, funny son from him? Yes, he had heard the statistics about deaths and missing children, and he had immediately googled the phenomenon which he had so unwittingly accepted as his current reality. There was no way anyone could ever willingly harm his kind, brave son. He was not even prepared to consider the worst implications of the situation.

Sharon and Harry couldn't have coaxed the information from the detective fast enough after he had admitted to having found something. Finding something is better than knowing nothing and continuing completely in the dark.

"They found Jamie's baseball cap in a trash can a few blocks away," said Detective Boyd. Sharon was visibly shaken, and Harry held her so tight that it seemed he was trying to hold them both together before they broke into little pieces. They had to stay strong for their son.

Harry made sure his wife would be fine standing on her own, and then asked to be taken immediately to the location where Jamie's hat was discovered. Two policemen were sifting through said trash can in search of further evidence and Harry was aware of officers going door-to-door looking for possible eyewitnesses.

He was permitted to stand in while the officers were questioning local residents, with instructions not to interfere, and that's what he did with every resident in the vicinity. He soon became discouraged with the same responses from so many. They were inside, watching television, in their bedrooms, eating. No one seemed to have been outside when Jamie's hat was discarded in the trash can. But how could that be so?

The officer Harry was shadowing was eventually done with interviewing. Harry took a break to calm down, still seething that witnesses had not been forthcoming in the area. The constant honking of car horns was making it decidedly difficult to concentrate, which was irritating him. It dawned on him that an inordinate traffic of vehicles seemed apparent and he considered his whereabouts and the reason behind the traffic on the road. Upon review, he realized that the road was a section of Interstate 195 and he formed a theory about what may have happened to his son. He demanded to be taken back to the school to speak with Detective Boyd immediately.

Jasper Joshua West

Chapter Five

"The office is calling for your dismissal, Kimberly," Mrs. Anderson announced before the whole class. Her voice snapped Kimberly out of a daydream, but she was just glad to be going home.

When Mrs. Anderson announced that she would be accompanying Kimberly, she became curious about the reason for a teacher's presence. Regardless of the odd condition that came with it, she was glad that she could go home and nap more comfortably.

As soon as the door closed to the classroom and they were alone in the hallway, the teacher's voice took on a sense of urgency, "It's an emergency, leave your things here and follow me." She proceeded to guide her towards the rear of the school and out the door which snapped shut behind her. Suddenly, Kimberly was all alone, searching out her mother's car so she could get herself home. She felt a sting on her neck and the world went dark.

Jasper Joshua West

Chapter Six

Back at the school, Harry jumped out of the police cruiser and demanded an audience with Detective Boyd. "Check the interstate!" Harry exclaimed when he regrouped with Boyd and his wife.

"We've alerted the State Police and they are looking for the vehicle on the interstate," said Boyd. "Now there is something that I need you to do to help. Could you get something that has Jamie's scent on in for the canine team?"

"Of course," Harry said, then turned to Sharon. "Will you be alright if I go home to get Jamie's favorite shirt, honey?"

"Yes, Harry, I'll be fine. Please just help them find our son as soon as they can."

Harry was escorted by the second-in-command, Officer Pearson, to their house. Harry walked in and went straight to Jamie's bedroom. Pearson followed and stood in the doorway.

"I know exactly what to use," Harry said, picking up Jamie's discarded pajamas from the floor. "These were his favorite pajamas, a gift from his uncle when they went to a Yankees game. They probably haven't been washed for a week or more," Harry said, holding up the navy-blue pajama top and pants covered in NY Yankees logos.

"That's perfect," Pearson said with a sad smile.

There was a silence between the two. Since when is finding your missing child's favorite pajamas something you get so excited about? Harry walked into his son's room again and looked around for a while, asking himself one question: If he ever saw his son again, what condition would he be in? The best-case scenario was that he was found happy and alive. Worst-case scenario was that he was found dead, murdered by someone who committed a senseless crime that would never be solved.

With his back to Pearson, Harry said, "I think some stranger has taken my son and is driving him God knows where on the interstate. I told your detective and he brushed it off. Are you going to brush it off?"

After a short pause, Pearson responded, "No, sir, I'm not. I have a daughter and I don't know what I would do in your position, probably go insane. I will do everything in my power to find your son."

Harry turned to Officer Pearson and they shared a moment as fathers, acknowledging the severity of the issue and how passionate they both were to solve the case and get Jamie safely home.

Taken

They smiled at each other and then got into the cruiser, to return to the school. Climbing out of the vehicle, Harry heard something through the radio that stopped him in his tracks. "... witness described a car that she saw a boy matching the given description getting into and leaving around the estimated time of the crime." Harry got out of the cruiser and said, "Find my boy," and Pearson nodded as he was pulling away to investigate the lead.

Jasper Joshua West

Chapter Seven

"We will keep you updated if-"

Boyd was cut off mid-sentence by an incoming phone call and raised a finger to indicate to Sharon that it was important. He listened intently, seemingly not wanting to miss a word of the call.

He quickly remarked, "We will be in touch very soon," and left, leaving Sharon with junior officers and the school principal. A minute or two later, Harry arrived and hugged his wife so tightly that it temporarily winded her.

"They might have an eyewitness who saw Jamie get into a car!" he told her. Looking into his eyes, his wife saw genuine excitement and the first real glimmer of hope since their son had gone missing.

Sharon hugged her husband as tightly as she possibly could and her eyes welled up with tears of joy as she whispered, "I love you, Harry. We're going to find him."

After the long, intimate hug, Harry grabbed Sharon's hand and led her out to his truck so they could contribute to the search for a car matching the witness's description. They met a team of officers at the SRTA terminal and offered to help in any way. They didn't need any help, so the two made their way to the next location, nearby. Once at the ferry pier, they separated to look around the parking lot.

After about ten minutes, just as Harry was about to suggest they give up and search somewhere else, he heard Sharon yell, "Over here!"

His heart started beating like a drum as he followed the sound of his wife's voice.

He rushed to her side and followed her line of vision to the inside of a car matching the unique description given. He saw what she was seeing: the shoes that Jamie was wearing that morning before he disappeared.

Chapter Eight

Jamie's eyes reluctantly opened to a sunny, blue sky. He saw the back of the strange, foreign woman from his dream. Or had it not been a dream? His thoughts were fuzzy, and the memories of the car ride were like a missing puzzle piece.

Becoming increasingly aware of his surroundings, he realized that he was gently rocking back and forth, making him slightly nauseous. He turned his head slightly and saw the sea and the fading shoreline. When he moved to stand up, the woman whipped her head around to face him and smiled.

"Shhh," she whispered, as his eyes became heavier, and he became all the more tired.

Jasper Joshua West

Chapter Nine

"Yes, this is Sharon and Harry Giles, calling from the State Pier Maritime Terminal. We found a car with our son's shoes inside, please come quick!"

Following Sharon's concise calls to both Detective Boyd and 911, the police showed up within 15 minutes and ran to the scene of their discovery.

They immediately gained access to the car and searched it thoroughly. When they were preparing to open the trunk, Harry and Sharon felt more fear than either had ever felt in their lives. What would they do if that trunk opened to reveal the corpse of their son staring back at them? What would their purpose in life be? If the trunk of that car exposed their son's lifeless corpse, they would both be very lost for a very long time; possibly forever.

The search of the backseat of the car revealed Jamie's shirt and the jeans he was wearing when he went missing. They also found the tags obviously hastily removed from the new clothes that Jamie would be wearing when they found him. Not if.

There had been some doubt at the start of the investigation that this was anything more than a child wandering off during school, but now it was crystal clear that it was a kidnapping.

Chapter Ten

"I can't believe they haven't found him yet. I thought we were so close. The longer it takes to find him, the less the chance we have of finding him alive," said Sharon with tears streaming down her face.

Harry replied, "We just have to keep faith that our boy will be found. We both know how smart and resourceful he is, Sharon." As he said this, he reached for her and wiped the tears from her face.

"I know, honey, it's just hard. Promise me that we will never stop looking for our baby," Sharon sobbed. Her voice was trembling but sure, as she put all of her frustrations, anger, and sadness into her request.

"I swear," Harry promised, his voice breaking on his words.

Even as they were having this conversation, both were experiencing doubt and fear. No matter how kind or smart Jamie was, the world is a harsh and cruel place, filled with monstrous, senselessly violent people. Even on the way to the police station to potentially get answers, it was hard to keep faith having had no communication with your missing child in more than a day.

When they arrived at the station, they were shocked to see FBI agents already there. Before they even had time to question this, Detective Boyd tracked them down and pulled them into a room to watch a surveillance video on a computer.

"We think that we have found your son boarding a boat with two adults this morning in this security footage. We would like you guys to take a second look," said the detective.

Harry's and Sharon's eyes grew wide and then Sharon let out a gasp. They were watching her son being half-dragged onto a boat by two strangers. Now that Sharon and Harry knew that their son was alive, they would stop at nothing to get him back.

Still recovering from the initial shock, they were approached by an FBI agent who said wearily, "Folks, your son is not the only child who has been taken."

Chapter Eleven

"I'm agent Harper, the lead investigator for an organized kidnapping ring that targets children. Unfortunately, Jamie has become a victim of this ring and he is one of many cases we are investigating.".

The look of disgust and shock on Sharon's face grew increasingly intense with every word that Agent Harper spoke. Sharon tightly gripped the arms of her chair with both hands, causing her knuckles to turn white while trying to process all the infuriating information she had just been told. Imagining several kids being drugged, kidnapped, and smuggled was somehow worse than seeing her child forcefully dragged onto the boat, drugged to the point that he was in and out of consciousness.

The FBI was not able to disclose every detail of the case, but they were able to explain the general overview of what they have gathered so far. There had been at least 20 recorded cases of kidnapping associated to this ring in the United States and Canada.

The culprits had always used the same method when initially abducting the children. Using a dart that had tranquilizing properties proportionate to children. They kidnapped the child and drove him or her to the nearest location for docking boats. Their knowledge ends just there on the typical patterns of the abductors.

Harper shows them into the room used for investigating the case, where Harry is immediately drawn to a map indicating all the locations struck by the criminals.

"They are abducting children near the east coast and heading south with them."

"That is our understanding too, sir. What we can't seem to figure out is why," said Harper.

Chapter Twelve

Stacey Jacobs huffed in frustration as the alarm sounded on her phone, reminding her to fetch Kimberly. She tended to become so focused on her drawings that the hours flew by without her noticing. She slammed her sketchbook closed and grabbed her keys out of a bowl on her vanity, picked up her purse, and checked her hair in the mirror before she walked out the door.

She stepped out and locked the door behind her, immediately donning her sunglasses. It was such a sunny day, enough to be almost unbelievable. She got into her car and made her way to her daughter's school to collect her.

When she arrived, Kimberly wasn't in her normal spot on the bench, waiting to be picked up after the school day. After waiting for about 20 minutes, Stacey began to become impatient and anxious about her daughter's tardiness. She decided to check whether she had been waiting in the office for some reason. She parked her car in front of the office and rang the doorbell, which got the attention of the secretary, who recognized her immediately and buzzed her in.

"Good afternoon, Melissa, has Kimberly been in here for the last few minutes?" Stacey asked as she quickly scanned the room for her daughter.

"No, Stacey, I haven't seen her, but let me check on her attendance today," replied the secretary as she typed Kimberly's name into her computer to search the database.

A few minutes later, a look of confusion dawned on Melissa's face as she spoke, "It says here that she was absent for all her classes this afternoon."

"That's impossible, I didn't pick her up," Stacey said, starting to panic. "Call 911 and report her missing," she said and ran for her car. She entered the address to the police station into her GPS and made her way over there to file a report. She had already lost valuable hours to find her daughter without even knowing she was gone.

Taken

Chapter Thirteen

"Step out with your hands up," yelled the officer. They had finally managed to locate the boat from the surveillance tape showing Jamie being dragged onto a dock. A man was found on board, but he scurried down to the cabin as soon as they began closing in. They heard him moving around in the cabin down below and then there was silence.

The officer climbed down the ladder with his hand resting on his gun holster in case he needed to use it to defend himself from whatever he might encounter at the bottom. Once off the ladder, he quickly scanned the area and found the man face-down and motionless on the ground.

He slowly approached him, putting two fingers on his neck to check for a pulse. Thankfully, he was breathing, so they could question him when he regained consciousness.

Taken

They searched for the woman and Jamie, but there was no sign of them. The only indication that they were ever there was the surveillance tape showing them forcing Jamie onto the boat. He let out a huff, frustrated that they couldn't interrogate the man immediately, and called Detective Boyd to give him an update.

"We found the boat, sir. The man was on board, but the woman and the kid are gone."

Chapter Fourteen

Jamie's eyes slowly opened for the third time as the strange, foreign woman shook him awake. She yanked him to his feet and pulled him by the arm along the metal floor of a narrow hallway. He tried as best he could to keep up with her, tripping over his own feet and struggling to make out the hallway through blurred vision.

After what seemed like forever, he felt himself being lifted, but he was far too weak to fight back and simply went limp in her arms. He looked down at the metal floor, confused as to why they might have stopped. Then she reached down and pulled on a lever beyond Jamie's line of vision, and they began descending a flight of stairs. He was so dizzy, and it was so hard to keep his eyes open. What had she done to him?

His eyes flew open in alarm when she set him down roughly on yet another metal floor. He took the chance to scan his surroundings to the best of his abilities. He first noticed a toilet in front of him. Just before his pants were pulled down and she yelled at him, leaving him in no doubt as to what she wanted him to do. All his fear and confusion erupted at once as he peed into the tiny, metal toilet, the dark color of his pee indicating that he was dehydrated. After urinating in the toilet at her command, he was led to the far end of the small, dingy room.

Scanning the room further, he made out about 5 sets of triple bunk beds. They all had mats but no blankets or pillows, which was fine with him because the room was extremely warm, cramped, and suffocating. She took him by the hand and guided him over to the beds, and he had his first sense of relief since being abducted; he would finally be allowed a chance to rest for a while. No more moving or waking up in strange places; he was finally settling down, even if it was in a scary and unfamiliar metal room with no privacy.

She lifted him again and set him down on a lower bunk before turning around and walking out. He couldn't stop thinking about how hungry he was - when was the last time he had eaten? He yearned for his mother's homemade fresh-baked, gooey chocolate chip cookies and a tall glass of cold milk.

While the hunger was gnawing away at him, he was glad to finally have a comfortable place to sleep. He tossed and turned until he was comfortable enough to let their tranquilizing drugs carry him away into sleep again.

Jasper Joshua West

Taken

Chapter Fifteen

"I have something," a coast guard pilot broadcast over the radio. He looked down to see a man frantically paddling a boat carrying two more passengers which had stalled.

"Nearby units on the water, move in," instructed the lead officer of the coast guard branch of the search unit of the investigation. Once the paddler was surrounded, he put up his hands in surrender while a woman quickly forced a child into the cabin below the deck of the boat.

"Come out with your hands up, ma'am," the lead officer shouted as he pulled his gun from its holster and held it at the ready. She appeared on the ladder with a scowl on her face, and his team proceeded to handcuff them as soon as she was back on deck. Two officers went below, and one returned with the motionless body of a young girl in his arms.

Taken

"Does she have a pulse?" the lead investigator asked the officer.

"Yes sir, but it is very faint, she needs to get to a hospital immediately."

The lead investigator signaled to him and he gently took the girl into his arms.

"Get back to shore as soon as possible," he barked at the officer who was tasked with taking the boat back to be searched in order to gather forensic evidence.

Boyd got news of the girl being found and just as he ended the call his phone rang again.

"Sir, we tried to make another arrest at a private dock where a boat had been stolen came back," said the frantic officer on the phone. "The suspect fired on us and we returned fire, killing him."

When the boat was about 15 minutes from the closest docking station, all the officers' radios went off simultaneously, all sounding the same transmission, "We found more abandoned boats in the area that may be related to this case. Do you want us to bring them back as well, sir?"

A grave look dawned on the officer in charge's face as he said, "Bring them all."

They were almost back at the docks when an officer from the second boat found said, "I have some bad news, sir. Our third arrest and one of our only leads just passed away."

Jasper Joshua West

Taken

Chapter Sixteen

It was 5:30 and there were already 42 kidnappings committed by these criminals, including only the cases that were actually reported. There had been no progress in the Jamie Giles case, with seemingly constant new questions to be asked, but absolutely no answers to be found.

Hundreds of qualified professionals, soldiers, and civilians compiled of law enforcement, military, and volunteer groups had been searching for leads for hours. The latest update received by Agent Harper was regarding the discovery of a few abandoned boats, that were the closest link to finding the missing children. There were dozens of children out there, lost and alone, and she could not stop thinking about it and picturing them. Hiding in dark rooms with tears in their eyes, not sure if or when they would be back home.

Taken

But the biggest question of all was: when they successfully kidnapped the children, where did they take them? The coast guard had boats and helicopters patrolling all the areas zoned for the recent kidnappings over the last few hours. Nothing had been found as yet. How had the children not been found on boats or islands? Any seaplanes given clearance for take-off would have been noticed and searched, so that wasn't their method of choice for transportation either.

When faced with so many possibilities in an investigation, it is usually best to eliminate them one by one and see which ones you are left with. The children were all kidnapped from schools, on land, and taken to boats in local marinas, each one paired with two handlers. Sometimes one handler brought the boat back to land alone and escaped, but other times the boat was abandoned. Where were the children being dropped off?

There was only one way for people to disappear in the middle of the sea, one last option to consider in this case: submarines.

Chapter Seventeen

"You guys have been looking for hours and you are supposed to be the best of the best!" Sharon exclaimed.

"Honey, they are doing their best, we have to let them do their jobs," Harry comforted although he had to admit that he felt the same way. They seemed to have gathered every law enforcement professional in the United States and Canada to investigate this ring, only to come up with some measly abandoned boats. Life was feeling more and more hopeless every hour without news on Jamie's or the kidnapped kids' whereabouts.

Where could these people hide dozens of scared, loud kids for 24 hours a day, 7 days a week, all at once without raising a single alarm or getting one complaint? Why did they always choose to travel by boat, and with two handlers instead of one? Could they be transporting the kids to an island not yet discovered? And why, if that was the case?

"We are trying our hardest, folks. We're really hoping that the abandoned boats will lead to some answers. There has to be a reason they operate the way they do," said Harper as she ran a hand down her face.

Sharon turned to Harper and saw all her desperation, fear, and frustration mirrored in her face, and immediately felt ashamed of herself. How could she stand there and accuse a woman of not being determined enough to search for her son when she was carrying the weight of all those missing children on her shoulders? She felt tears in her eyes as she hugged Harper, silently acknowledging that they were going through this nightmare together, sharing the long days, sleepless nights, and tears. As she looked up at Harper, she saw that tears were forming in her eyes as well and gave her one last squeeze before she stepped back to stand next to her husband.

"I'm sorry, Harper, I know this must be stressful for you, too. I just miss my son," a sob rose out of Sharon's throat.

"It's alright, ma'am, I know this process can be painful. We really are using every resource we have at our disposal to bring down this ring and bring these kids home safe," Harper said.

"I just hope you solve the case before it's too late – for both Jamie and for those other kids they took," said Harry.

Jasper Joshua West

Chapter Eighteen

Stacey had been sitting in the small, suffocating police station for the last two hours, waiting for any word on her daughter's whereabouts. The little makeup that she'd had the time to put on while she was on the way out had streaked down her face and dried hours ago. Her impatience started to boil over again as she started to make her way over to the desk where she initially reported her daughter's disappearance.

"Have you heard anything about my daughter? Her name is Kimberly Jacobs and she has already been missing for hours," Stacey asked the woman working at the front desk.

The receptionist answered, "I'm sorry, ma'am, we've got people out looking for your daughter-" She was cut off mid-sentence by the shrill ring of her phone, which she then answered.

"We found a young girl matching the description provided for Kimberly. I am sending an email with an attached photograph of her over now. We need the mother to confirm that it is her daughter. If she's sure that's her daughter, bring her to Memorial Hospital."

Before she could even utter 'yes ma'am' in response, the officer hung up the phone.

The receptionist turned back to Stacey and said, "Ma'am, I need you to confirm that the young lady in this photo is your daughter," and beckoned her closer so they could see the computer monitor.

"Yes, that's her! Where is she? Is she alright?" Stacey was beyond relieved that her daughter was alive. Tears of happiness began to stream down her face as she imagined her reunion. She would never take her daughter for granted again; she would cherish every second they had together.

"I see her now. We will be on our way soon, sir," an officer spoke into his phone as he headed towards Stacey from of an office in the back. He smiled at Stacey as he removed the phone from his ear and pressed the end call button. When he reached her, he extended his arm and opened his hand for her to shake, and she obliged happily with a big smile on her face.

"Hello, ma'am, I'm Officer Cyrus and I will be escorting you to the hospital to see your daughter this afternoon," said the officer. With a quick 'follow me', he led her to his cruiser and within a matter of minutes they were on their way to the hospital where her daughter was a patient.

About 15 minutes later, they arrived at the hospital and Officer Cyrus immediately escorted Stacey to her daughter's room. Stacey's face lit up as soon as she saw her. Although Kimberly looked as if she was just taking a nap, Stacey knew that her daughter was unconscious. Even with that knowledge at that time, she cringed when she saw the small, red irritated patch on her daughter's skin that indicated that she had been drugged.

"She's one of the lucky ones – she made it back home safe," said Officer Cyrus.

Jasper Joshua West

Chapter Nineteen

Harper woke up to the ringtone she had specifically set temporarily to the tone of an alarm clock, so she was assured to always be woken by it ringing. She specifically changed it during this case for one reason – she had been having trouble sleeping, and when she was able to, the loud ringing was barely audible to her. On the rare occasion that she was able to sleep, nightmares about darts and crying children in dark rooms, especially Jamie, woke her only 10 minutes into her power naps.

"Ma'am, he just woke up," the officer said. Harper was extremely proud of the bright junior officer for arresting Kimberly's kidnappers. His first big arrest. He managed to detain two criminals in one of the most notorious cases of organized crime in the last decade, and his name would never be forgotten.

"I'm on my way. Bring both suspects into the interrogation room and do not let anybody you don't know into that room or I will have your badge," replied Harper sternly. Although she was proud of his big arrest, sometimes an officer rising through the ranks and receiving so much attention so quickly needed to be humbled.

She quickly threw on her uniform and grabbed her badge from her bedside table. Was it wrong that this was the most alive that she had felt in months? She loved being in the middle of the action of a case, along with the anticipation that came with getting answers from the lowest of the low. She hated being sidelined when she was a rookie, being told not to interfere and stand in the corner when all she wanted was to take over the handling of the interrogation herself.

She was walking through the old, creaky doorway of the police station 20 minutes later, greeted with 'good morning' from all directions. She smiled and nodded at every officer who greeted her. She had built her career very carefully, always demanding respect and an acknowledgment of her authority from her inferiors, but always showing them the same respect and acknowledging their hard work and dedication. Taking this approach her entire career had always earned her their support and helped her make some genuine lifelong friends.

She walked through the door into the interrogation room and sneered as her eyes fell on the two perpetrators. They both wore smug smiles and were tapping the table with the same simultaneous and monotonous tempo. The man's teeth were filthy. An unhealthy shade of yellow that Harper had never even seen on a human being before, they were uneven and severely chipped. Her eyes moved to the woman and she gasped softly. She was beautiful, the polar opposite of her partner.

"Stop that," Harper snapped, concluding eventually that their consistent tapping was not playing the role of Morse code. Their smug smiles only widened in response. She was momentarily reminded of the Cheshire cat as she watched their smiles grow.

"So, you make your living kidnapping kids for some scumbag?" she asked them. At first, they didn't respond, but when Harper slammed her hand on the table in front of them and yelled, "Answer me," the woman snapped back in a language Harper had no trouble instantly recognizing as Russian. Harper started to ask herself why this Russian woman was helping a kidnapping ring? Then she registered that this was much bigger than they thought – this ring originated in Russia and may well be operating from within Russia. Her case just became an international issue, and with the tension already high between the United States and Russia, that was very dangerous. Very dangerous, indeed.

That was when she noticed the faint outline of a clear capsule protruding from behind each of their ears. Two Russians trying to kidnap a little girl in the United States, with pills behind their ears immediately after they were captured? It was clear that this interview wasn't going to go anywhere until they found a Russian translator, and maybe not even then.

Harper walked over to the junior agent who was guarding the door and whispered in his ear, "They both have capsules full of cyanide. They are going to try off themselves as soon as this interrogation ends because they are far more afraid of their handlers than they are of us. We can't let that happen, can we?"

"No ma'am," he said with a determined look, much to her delight. He quickly darted over to the Russian prisoners and grabbed the poorly concealed pills from their resting spots behind the ears and handed them to his superior. Harper smiled as they started yelling in Russian, glaring at them with mean eyes, no doubt showering them with every insult they could think of.

"We're done here, thank you for your cooperation," Harper quipped as she walked out of the interviewing room, now the one with a smug smile on her face.

Chapter Twenty

Agent Harper and Detective Boyd nodded at each other as they walked into the secure room designated to meeting about the case. They were joined by all Agent Harper and Detective Boyd's superiors, military personnel, and the Secretary of Defense. They scanned the room for their names and sat down in the seats assigned to them as signified by their name tags on the long oval-shaped table. Harper had just picked up her case briefing packet when the director of the FBI cleared his throat.

"Good morning and welcome. You all know why you are here. We need to secure this ring before they cause an international incident," he said. He scanned the room as he spoke, watching the reactions as he emphasized the international implications of the incident. He was met with nervous expressions from all in attendance who were worried about the latent consequences. – War was the worst-case scenario. The United States and Russia did not need more reason for hostility, walking on eggshells as they already were.

"We have an update on their movements. They started kidnapping children in South America as of last week. Same MO as the other kidnappings – they abduct the kids while they are at recess, quickly and quietly. We need to stop this now, too many kids are missing and too many questions can't be answered. Are there any questions?" asked the director.

"Sir, have we found out which drug they used in the tranquilizer?" the junior officer who arrested the Russians asked and Harper smiled.

He was the only person in the room who was not high-ranking in any law enforcement agency. As the person who had captured the only handlers still in possession of a victim, doors were now opened for him, offering opportunities he would otherwise not have seen for years to come.

"The rookie has a good question! Yes, we have, and we are investigating where they may have purchased it," said the director.

As he opened his mouth to say more, his phone began to vibrate and then went on to ring loudly on the table before him. He huffed in annoyance, but his eyes widened when he saw his phone screen.

He held up a finger as he uttered, "Excuse me, I have to take this."

He cleared his throat and picked up his cell phone with hands trembling slightly.

He answered the call with a, "Hello sir, do we have an update?" and listened intently to everything said on the other end of the line until he eventually hung up.

He turned to everyone in the room with a serious expression and said, "That was the president of the United States. It's time for the American people to know what's happening."

Chapter Twenty-One

The president replaced the receiver having ended his phone call to the director, with a grave look on his face. It was up to him to hold the first press conference on the new kidnapping ring operating throughout the United States and Canada. He had never liked press conferences, but he knew this one was going to be especially hectic. The media would simply not stand for this. He could hear them now: "Children taken in broad daylight from schoolyards. I've never heard of such a thing! How could the teachers let this happen? How could you continue to let this happen?"

Whenever a disaster occurs, even the most drastically different of people seem to react similarly; blaming everybody except those who are committing the heinous crimes. When it comes down to it, pointing their fingers at him and blaming him seemed their chosen defense mechanism. As if he would have been able to save those poor children. God knows where they are and what those savages have done to them.

He tried his best to clear his head. He cleared his throat and stepped into the room full of reporters. Every single one of them waiting for his comment so they could twist it into whatever completely different meaning they concocted to that intended. He scanned the room and flinched as the camera flashes went off. He had learned a long time ago, long before he was ever elected president, to look at a room full of people before addressing them and if they see you acknowledge them. It makes them feel more respected and more confident in what you have to say. He was definitely acknowledging them. He seemed to be surrounded by a group of bloodthirsty hounds who wouldn't stop their attack until they had the answers they wanted to hear. God, he hated press conferences.

"Good morning, ladies and gentlemen. I trust you have already heard rumors about all the recent kidnappings being somehow related. Unfortunately, these rumors have merit to them," said the president. The room resounded with gasps and exclamations of surprise, although they had all been quite aware of this information before coming into the conference. He always wondered about the purpose behind them pretending that they were receiving new information. What he knew for sure was that he would probably never know.

"Please settle down. We have reason to believe that the main conspirators behind this operation are from a foreign country. All the criminals we have arrested in connection with this crime speak fluent Russian," he said. He knew ahead of time that the room would be filled with cries of outrage and angry curses when he made this particular announcement , and he assumed correctly. One woman even spat on the floor, which frankly was a little excessive, in his opinion.

"They have only targeted children during school recess so far, and only children sitting by themselves. We have to make sure that we are keeping our children as safe as possible by keeping them together in groups whenever they are out of the classroom, no matter where they are going or the time of day," he announced.

He took a deep breath and then said, "As of yesterday one of the girls has been returned safely home to her mother." He anticipated he would be met with applause even before they started clapping. They may very well have thrived off negative information, but they could nonetheless not help but be grateful for the recovery of a child. The smile that had grown on his face disappeared as soon as it had come when he prepared his next announcement.

"Although it is wonderful that we reunited one family, there are still dozens of broken families out there that need answers and want their children back. We are continuing to investigate and will hold another conference when we have further updates. Thank you and have a nice day." Walking out of the room, he felt the familiar relief that comes only at the conclusion of a press conference.

He turned to his aide who was walking with and gravely said, "We have to find those kids before there is nothing left of them to find."

Chapter Twenty-Two

Stacey leaned forward in the seat that she had hours ago relocated to beside her daughter's hospital bed. She was getting more worried about Kimberly by the second. Was she supposed to be slipping in and out of consciousness at this point? She squeezed her hand, silently wishing that it would bring her daughter out of her prolonged unconsciousness and see her smile at her. Her heart started to beat like a drum when her daughter's hand began to twitch under hers, and her eyes widened in surprise.

Kimberly looked up and whimpered, "Mommy?"

"Honey? I'm here, Mommy's here."

Kimberly slowly opened her eyes and when she saw her mother, tears started to well in her eyes. Stacey gently wrapped her arms around her daughter, wishing she could hold her in her arms every minute of every day for all eternity. One thing was for sure. She was never losing her daughter again. She would take her out of the school and transfer her to one she trusted. Or even home school her, if that's what it came to.

She suddenly remembered that she promised to call Officer Cyrus the second Kimberly woke up and started talking. She pulled his card out of her purse and carefully dialed his number.

"She's awake, she just woke up and started talking to me," she blurted. She was sure to add the fact that she had spoken having already called 3 times before today. Three times that had turned out to be false alarms.

"I'm on my way now, Stacey. Keep her talking and comfortable," the officer blurted, the sound of rustling in the background as he picked up the key to his cruiser. Ending the phone call, she gently caressed Kimberly's face.

"How are you feeling, sweetie?"

"My head hurts, Mommy. Can we go home?" asked Kimberly, whimpering as she spoke.

"Not yet, baby, a nice man is going to come and ask you questions. After we talk to him, we have to wait for the nurse to say that it's alright."

Officer Cyrus entered Kimberly's hospital room, interrupting the small talk between mother and daughter. Stacey had not wanted to over extend her before the questioning began.. The officer smiled and nodded at her and then extended his hand out to her daughter.

"You must be Kimberly! I've heard so much about you from your mom," he spoke as she reached for his hand and shook it. Then she waved her hand and tried to hide her face behind her mom's hand. She had always been nervous around strangers, even before this recent ordeal.

"Do you remember anything from the last day, sweetie?" he asked. When he saw the look of confusion dawn on her face, he already knew what was coming.

"I don't remember, I'm sorry," Kimberly sobbed as her mother held her and whispered sweet words of reassurance in her ear.

Taken

Chapter Twenty-Three

During the drive back to the station Harper tried to wrap her mind around the idea of the ring kidnapping even more kids from new places. The director was right, there were too many unanswered questions and too many people looking to them for answers for them to not have any to give. At that point, the president had to get involved. Hopefully, Sharon and Harry hadn't seen his press conference yet. She wanted to be the one to tell them about finding Kimberly.

She sighed and momentarily closed her eyes and rested her head on the steering wheel before taking the keys out of the ignition. As she climbed out of the car, she couldn't stop thinking about the news she was just given, imagining what it would be like when the number of missing children rose into the hundreds. Why were these people kidnapping innocent children, and what did they want? She was still trying to come up with answers as she walked into the police station.

Sharon immediately stood when she saw Harper walk into the room, and blurted out, "What happened? Did you find him?" The desperation in her eyes and her voice almost brought Harper to tears; this woman was depending on her to bring her son home safe and sound, and she wasn't even sure if she was capable of taking care of herself at that point.

When Harry saw the look on Harper's face, he grabbed his wife's hand before she even had a chance to answer, and said, "I don't think so, honey. Not yet."

Harper could see him losing more and more hope every time she saw him. Losing hope of ever seeing his son again and in the justice system as a whole; losing hope that Harper could do her job.

"We didn't find Jamie, but we did find another student being held captive by two criminals, and we have detained them." said Harper. Although this wasn't the news that they were hoping for, a glimmer of hope shone in their eyes and Harper knew why; they would finally get some answers. After so many sleepless nights, wondering if their son was dead or alive, they would finally find out what these people wanted with him What they were doing and what they were planning to do with him.

"She is unconscious in the hospital right now, but one of our agents will ask her questions as soon as she wakes up." Harper assured them.

Sharon stepped forward towards Harper as she said, "Thank you for everything you have done for us. I don't know what we would have done if we didn't have you in our corner."

She had such a genuine smile on her face that it made Harper's sides ache. There was a real possibility that this woman would never see her son again and that it would break both their hearts. That was one of her rules. No getting personally invested in a case. Especially one like this, where the light at the end of the tunnel seemed not to exist and they would be in the dark forever.

"Of course, ma'am," replied Harper, having to make a conscious effort to keep her voice from shaking. As she smiled back at Sharon, she couldn't help feeling guilty. They had no idea where her son was or what was being done to him, and they probably wouldn't for a while.

"We are seeing a consistent pattern of two abductors taking the children onto boats that have been abandoned at sea. When they return the boat to a different marina, the children and one of the perpetrators are gone," said Harper. She was met with two expressions of confusion and continued with the update she was permitted to give them.

Taken

"At this point, we are unsure where the children are being taken to or dropped off. It honestly just seems like they are being dropped into the middle of the ocean." "Maybe they are being held in another larger boat until their captors have enough for whatever they are planning. Then they could be transporting them to an island or crossing the US border," offered Harry. One look into his desperate, tired eyes clearly indicated just how close to snapping he was and how near he was to a breakdown. That was assuming he hadn't had one already.

"Maybe," said Harper, trying to sound as confident as possible, even though she doubted that his theory was accurate. She already had a theory of her own, but yet another of her rules was never to share unconfirmed information with anyone. This could not only get her into trouble, but also hurt them if she was wrong. Sharing inaccurate information could be dangerous.

"There are very few ways they could be holding the kids after they have been dropped off in the ocean. They would need a place for them to eat and sleep and living quarters where they can also avoid detection," Harper thought out loud. Sharon shook her head and ran her hand down her face in frustration, failing to figure out what Harper was implying.

"Sharon, Harry, I think you guys should sleep in a hotel tonight. It is unsafe to keep sleeping at your house. They could know where you live and have you under surveillance or even attack you," warned Harper.

"We have to stay. What if Jamie escapes and comes home?" asked Sharon, the desperation returning to her voice.

Harry squeezed his wife's hand, "Honey, maybe she's right. It could be dangerous to stay at our house, and we won't be any good to Jamie if these people make us disappear too."

Sharon nodded as tears filled her eyes, and she turned to her husband.

"You're right, " she agreed.

"We'll go to a hotel for now, if that's what you think would be best, Harper," she whispered.

Harper smiled in response to her consent and thanked her for agreeing.

"You won't regret it, ma'am, a hotel is the safest place for you to be living right now."

"Call me Sharon."

Taken

Chapter Twenty-Four

"Detain all who are in your custody and have them taken to the location, and use the protocol we discussed," the president instructed over the phone. He made sure to disclose the location to the director in private because their phone line could easily be tapped, especially if the head of this ring was Russian. They were notorious for hacking into phones from across international waters, and their hackers would have no problem listening in to the president's phone calls.

After hearing the beeping sound that indicated the end of the phone call, he set his phone down on his desk and audibly sighed in exasperation. The same questions had been running through his head since he had attended the first briefing on this case.

Who were these people? What did they want with these innocent children they were kidnapping? Although one question in particular refused to leave the forefront of his mind; was this a Russian tactic to goad him into declaring war?

If it was, it would not work. Although this case was serious, he was not going to allow millions of US civilians and soldiers to be murdered in another war. Although the United States would probably eventually win, too many lives would be lost on both sides for him to ever be able to live with the decision.

The 'protocol' they had discussed was to use any resource at their disposal to get the Russians to talk. If it took torture, truth serum, a lie detector, or simply effective interrogative techniques, he would not walk into the next press conference without additional information.

During his campaign and consequent election, he always promised the American people one thing and that was that he would be effective by whatever means necessary. His legacy would be one to be respected for the right answers, not for cheating on his wife or making unfair treaties and agreements with other countries. He would be fair to countries who treated the US fairly, and harsh and swift with those who disrespected and threatened the US.

The manner in which this case was handled would no doubt partly shape his legacy and prove to be among his most remembered achievements. They needed answers and they needed them quickly.

"The transfer of the prisoners was successful. They wouldn't talk with normal interrogation methods, but we have resorted to the other strategies we discussed, and they are responding. We are about to gain more intel on this case," the director said in a phone call some two hours later.

Taken

Chapter Twenty-Five

Jamie groaned softly as his eyes slowly opened and he scanned his surroundings. He rubbed his eyes and looked around again. Where was he? He felt sluggish and it was a chore to even keep his eyes open long enough to get a clear view of the room.

"They must have injected me with another needle," he thought. He was getting used to the feeling of being constantly drugged and waking up in strange places.

He remembered when his parents had taken him on a trip to Florida and told him they would be flying in an airplane. He wasn't even entirely sure what an airplane was, but when they were boarding, he felt the panic set in. They were traveling in a huge machine with wings. In the sky for hours. Just thinking about all the potential disasters that could occur made his stomach hurt. Could this be an airplane? He certainly felt the same panic and, from what he was able to make out, there were similarities.

Then he saw them – sets of bunk beds all around the room already occupied by other children, all of who were asleep. He tried to focus well enough to count the number of bunk beds, but he couldn't. Dozens of kids were sleeping in the room. As he continued scanning the room, his eyes stopped on a tall woman holding a gun in her hand. He turned towards her and squinted to the point he thought she might be unable to tell that he was awake.

She turned her head to the side as another guard came into view who silently imparted some communication in sign language. Jamie had seen people use American sign language and this was not it. They were communicating using sign language from another country. He felt another wave of fear as he came to the realization that these people were not from the United States. The people who had kidnapped all these children were from a foreign country, but which one?

He suddenly realized that his bladder was full and that he had to use the bathroom. As the second guard left the room, he considered asking the woman watching them if he could use the bathroom, but he changed his mind. He was far too scared to get her attention, let alone ask for anything, especially seeing that she was holding a gun. He decided to hold it in until he had an opportunity to ask someone else or until she left the room, which was unlikely. He resigned himself to the fact that he would probably have to go to the bathroom right there, on that uncomfortable bed.

What happened to lead him to this point from sitting on the playground to being locked in a room full of kids with a gun trained on him? If he wasn't even safe sitting alone in the corner of a playground, could he ever be safe anywhere? He thought about how frantic his parents must be – their son having vanished from school during recess without so much as a sign of him since. No ransom call, no demands, no answers. After he felt the prick in his neck at recess, he vaguely remembered waking up in a strange car with strangers, and now waking up here.

Too many blocks of time were unaccounted for since that day on the playground. Was the car a dream, just the result of the drugs he was being injected with or was it all real? He was still contemplating what was fake and what was reality when he gave in to sleep, allowing his eyes to close.

Jamie felt himself start to come to again as he licked his dry and cracked lips, craving water. He slowly realized that he still needed to use the bathroom and he couldn't hold it in. It was either happening in the bathroom or right there in that bed. After taking a few minutes to build up the courage, he was prepared to ask the woman where he should go to find a toilet.

"Where is the b-bathroom?" he stuttered. She immediately whipped her head in his direction when she heard his voice and sneered at him. He cowered on his bunk as she slowly walked towards him, seemingly getting angrier with every step. When she reached him, she gripped his arm tightly and started dragging him across the metal floor while he tripped over his own feet trying to stay upright.

She finally released him in front of a short white door which she opened, pushing him towards the doorway. He was still looking around inside the dark room when the guard switched the light on and slammed the door behind him. He suddenly remembered that the airplane he had flown on to Florida also had a toilet. Did they bring him on another plane? While using the bathroom facilities, he looked at the walls and saw odd words and symbols he had never seen before. He shook it off and walked out of the bathroom, immediately coming face-to-face with the guard.

"Where did you take me? Where are my mommy and daddy?" he exclaimed while she stared at him with disdain in response.

"Go," she said in a very strange accent and pushed him out of the doorway and towards the room full of bunk beds. He allowed himself to be led to his bunk and there he lay down. He felt both relief and a fresh bout of fear wash simultaneously over him as he lay down and allowed sleep to carry him away again.

Jasper Joshua West

Taken

Chapter Twenty-Six

"Is it true that we have new information?" asked the FBI director as he quickly scanned the room for bugs, as was his norm. Even though some rooms were supposedly secure, crazier things had happened than merely a breach. This case was gaining traction, creating a global issue, just as they feared it would. He looked around the table and put the names of the agencies to faces; the CIA, Homeland Security, the Coast Guard, and even some unfamiliar faces.

"Yes, we have obtained a satellite video that we believe shows the movements of this ring," the head of the CIA said.

The television mounted on the wall in the front of the room suddenly came to life and everybody turned to face it. There was a grainy image of the beginning of a video showing a boat on the ocean.

"Was there a child on this boat?" asked the director of the Coast Guard, with a grimace.

The head of the CIA replied, "Yes, to our knowledge, a child was on this boat at the time this footage was caught."

He silently nodded and pressed play on the remote in his hand.

The video began with the boat silently speeding along the water for a few seconds and then suddenly coming to a halt in the middle of the open sea. Then a woman appeared, carrying a motionless child and handing him off to a person that was outside of the camera's view. It looked like she was dropping the child into the sea, but there was no way they would risk getting caught only to kill them in the long run. Everyone in the room seemed to have the same confused expression and to be thinking the same thing; what was going on here?

"Submarines have been identified on both the East and West coast, both being used to store these children and to stay on the move deep under water to avoid detection." He cleared his throat and continued, "We have reliable intel that they are using stolen boats to meet their handlers in the gulf-of-Mexico. They are following a pattern here and we have finally figured it out, now we need to find the kids."

He continued, "Judging by the position of this sighting, we are assuming they are headed towards South America. They could have gone just about anywhere, but we think that they most likely went to a country that can be reached by submarine."

"My god, Harper was right," muttered the director of the FBI.

A grave look crossed his face as he said, "We have another video that you need to see from a few months ago."

He pressed the play button for a second time and a video played showing a group of kids sitting on the deck of a boat surrounded by armed guards who were scanning the perimeter.

After he stopped the video and turned off the television, he flicked the light switch back on and looked around the room. He was met with scared and confused faces which now looked even more determined to catch these people.

"This is footage from the Panama kidnappings, and although the children were taken by boat rather than a submarine, we have strong reason to suspect that these two cases are related. We believe that these victims were taken to Columbia to either be sold into the sex-trade or be illegally adopted by rich families." "We also believe that these kids will meet the same fate if we do not find them. Relay all this information to your agents and find them." he said with a sense of urgency.

Chapter Twenty-Seven

Harry reached for his nightstand to press the snooze button on his blaring alarm clock. He ran his hand down his face and he was filled with dread, internally preparing to face another day without his son. He gently climbed out of bed, trying not to fully wake his wife.

"Go back to bed, sweetie," he whispered when he saw her start to stir. She grabbed his hand for a few seconds and then turned her back to him.

He slicked his hair back on his way to the bathroom and rinsed his face in the sink. Later, he washed his hands and softly closed the door. As he walked to the kitchen, his thoughts were on his morning coffee. Coffee had become somewhat of an antidote whenever he was hurting. Taking the first sip, he checked his voicemails and text messages for any updates. He was disappointed but not surprised to find neither.

He grabbed a notepad and pencil from the breakfast table and began his to-do list for the day. That was how he had been getting through the last few days. Writing a list of things to do helped him get through the hard days. He gripped the pencil tightly as he carefully wrote 'Contact Panama police.'

"Good morning, honey," said Sharon as she hugged her husband from behind. They both savored the sweet moment in the middle of the chaos for a few seconds.

"Good morning," Harry replied as he turned towards her to see tears starting to pool in her eyes.

"They are never going to find him, Harry. He disappeared days ago, and they haven't brought our baby back to us yet." "Don't say that, honey. They will find him, they're doing their best. They already have so many different leads that they are following. We will always keep looking, no matter what happens," Harry assured his wife. As his wife turned to him with a hopeful look on her face, he squeezed her hand, reassuring her that he would always be there.

"We will never stop," she replied in agreement. "I'm so glad that they have made so much progress so quickly. Finding Jamie seemed so impossible when he first disappeared. Thank God a nine-year-old boy disappearing into thin air brought everybody on the right side of the law together."

"They have made so much progress in so little time. I have a feeling that the connection between this case and the Panama abductions could be the key to solving this case. I know it has been three days already, but they will find him. We will find him, honey," he replied.

Their conversation was cut short when Harry's phone screen lit up with Agent Harper's name and rang. He answered the call and immediately put it on speaker so his wife could hear what Harper had to say.

"Hello, Harry. I have good news and bad news," said Harper nervously. Tears started to well up in Sharon's eyes when she heard the last few words, and Harry grabbed her hand, silently offering his support and presence.

"I'll give you the bad news first. There are no more updates on the locations of the submarines, they could be anywhere at this point. We also have definite confirmation that the drug used on the girl is from Russia. We were holding out hope that the ring hadn't originated in Russia, but it is already affecting foreign relations." Harry looked into his wife's eyes and knew that they were both just thankful that they hadn't found their son's body. The fact that they had lost track of the submarines was discouraging, but at least he was still presumed to be on it.

"The good news is that I was able to get that phone number we discussed. I will text you the number of the lead investigator of the Panama abduction cases after this phone call. Hopefully, he can help shed light on the solution for all of us," finished Harper.

"Thank you so much," said Sharon.

"Of course. I will update you if there are more changes," Harper added before hanging up.

A few minutes after the call ended, he received the text from Harper with the detective's phone number and immediately wrote it down on his list. As soon as he set his pencil down, he picked up his phone and dialed the number.

He shared a hopeful look with his wife as the phone rang – once, twice, and then stopped.

"This is Detective Ramos." "This is Harry and Sharon, Jamie's parents. Harper said she would tell you about us ahead of time. Please tell me you can help us find our son," begged Harry.

Chapter Twenty-Eight

Jamie's eyes hesitantly opened once again and he scanned his surroundings, trying to figure out whether or not he had been moved again. His eyes stopped on the familiar bunk beds that filled the room. He was definitely in the same place that he had fallen asleep. He turned to the bunk across from him and rubbed his eyes to help him focus. He gasped when he realized children were no longer asleep on the other bunks.

He turned in the bed to go back to sleep, when he was suddenly jerked upright, face-to-face with the odd-looking woman who had kidnapped him. She took him by the shoulder and pushed him towards a man he had never seen before. The man squeezed his shoulder and gently pushed him down a strange corridor with a metal floor, following behind armed with a hand gun.

Metal floors were everywhere. This wasn't like the airplane he remembered. He turned to face the man halfway down the corridor and felt an odd semblance of peace. For the first time in days he was finally with someone who wasn't yelling at him, hurting him, or poking him with needles.

"We see other kids now," the heavily accented man announced similarly to the accents Jamie had been hearing among the others.

Jamie immediately scanned the room as he was pushed over the threshold into a new area. Then he saw them – all the kids he had seen on the first night who had been asleep in the bunks, and then some, all sitting on a carpet together. They all seemingly turned their heads towards him when he walked into the room. At first, he thought they were looking at him, but when he turned around as well, it was to see a smiling woman carrying juice boxes and peanut butter and jelly sandwiches. He felt his stomach start to rumble as he asked for a sandwich, his voice just part of a sea of pleas around the room. After he gulped down two juice boxes and two sandwiches, he felt full and comfortable enough to ask questions.

"Where are we?" he asked the man who had led him into the room, only to be met with a silent response.

"Do you guys know where we are?" he asked the other children, but they didn't have answers for him either. He was met with wide confused eyes and murmurs of, 'I don't know.'

Taken

"I have an announcement," the strangely accented man addressed everyone from the front of the room. All heads turned to him as he spoke, all waiting for the answers they had been longing for.

"You will get off soon and get on a boat, then see your parents," he continued.

Jasper Joshua West

Chapter Twenty-Nine

"There it is! Flash our lights at them and give them a chance to surrender," commanded the Fleet Admiral.

The pride he felt at that moment was impossible to explain. His crew had been the first to find a submarine. Although he did warn them not to use force immediately, he secretly wished that they could. Who did these people think they were, coming into his country and terrorizing the nation? They had been so meticulous and careful to avoid getting caught, but they were about to feel the consequences of their actions.

It was a miracle that they were able to detect the submarine in the first place as it fled to Russia, which is why they were in a hurry, presumably. They were not expecting one of their puppets to be captured, and it scared them. So here they were, cornered trying to escape using the long route around the tip of South America. More games – they loved playing games.

"Fire, but do not directly hit it, there are children on board," he said as they shot one torpedo into the dark sea directly under the submarine. And then it started. The sub started moving faster, trying to get away, and he smiled. Now they were really getting started.

"After them," he screamed, spotting the cave they were headed or before they did. They noticed too late to avoid it or stop and the sub kept going, straight into their trap.

"Surrender now, there is no escape. We have you cornered. Rise to the surface or we will have to use deadly force," he demanded over the radio.

"You will not do it with children on board," replied a man in a clear Russian accent.

"Show them just how serious we are. Only shoot at the side. Do not do enough damage to harm anyone onboard," the Admiral instructed his crew.

The torpedo hit the side of the submarine, and the Russian urged, "Stop this! We are coming up, do not shoot anymore!"

As the foreign submarine began to rise to the surface, so did they, readying their firearms in the event of a worst-case scenario. A shootout.

Taken

A sniper on top of the boat aimed his firearm at the opening of the submarine as it surfaced, and the door slowly opened. A man emerged off a ladder and put his hands in the air as he stepped onto the slick surface of the submarine.

"Go, go, go! Find those kids," the admiral commanded.

"Get everyone into the conference room and put me on camera, it's time to tell them what we found," commanded the officer.

As the conference room filled again with officials, the stress and tension were like a dark cloud over all. They had all the important information for this case and the need for its urgency, but they had yet to yield any actual results. The director hated to admit it, but they were good at what they did. Avoiding detection once again, just when the Coast Guard thought they had them backed into a corner was no easy feat.

The desperation for answers was shown on every single face in the room; everybody hoping somebody else had found something. When somebody at the front of the room loudly cleared their throat, everybody focused their attention to the front of the room and the television screen showing a representative of the US Navy appearing from within a secure room.

"We found a submarine maneuvering around the tip of South America on its way to Russia. The vessel has surfaced, and we are currently waiting for the all-clear. CIA and Homeland personnel need to get here now," he declared amidst a round of applause in response.

"Don't celebrate too soon. This isn't over just yet. At least one submarine is still out there, maybe two. We are questioning the prisoners, but they are hard to break. This will not end until all the kids are found and every single man and woman in this ring are put behind bars. Keep working."

Chapter Thirty

"So many children were kidnapped and never found. We searched for months but it was as if they had simply vanished into thin air. There was no trace of them or any solid leads to follow," Harry's heart sank at the detective's admission.. They never found them, and they had just given up. Is that what would happen with his son?

"We are confident that these cases are related and with these new leads, we are also confident that we will find all the children missing from the three countries," assured detective Ramos.

"Thank you very much, detective," Harry said. Sharon stared, transfixed on the phone, her mind running a million miles an hour to process what she had just heard.

"Of course, sir. We will find your son and prosecute these people to the fullest extent of the law, that is a promise." Sharon squeezed her husband's hand, filled with renewed hope. Another country added to the search.

As Harry hung up, he managed to force a smile for the sake of his wife. They gave up in Panama, would they give up here if they didn't find the answers they were looking for? No matter how many assurances he got from agents or detectives, he had no guarantee that they would find his son.

Then it hit him like a semi-truck: he had to help in person. He would never be able to live with himself if he wasn't there doing all he could to help find his son.

"Honey, I have to help them to find our son. I can't just sit around here while he is out there, scared and alone," Harry said. He gently took his wife's hand with a sad but determined look in his eyes.

"Don't do this, Harry. Let the police do their job. They are trained for this and they know how to find our son," begged Sharon.

"I'm going, Sharon. You need to stay here in case Jamie comes home. The cops have to follow the law. I will do whatever it takes, break whatever rule I need to."   "No way I'll let you go alone. I'm going with. My sister can watch the house and stay updated with the police here. She will take care of things," Sharon decided.

"Are you sure you want to do this?" Harry asked hesitantly.

"I want to find our son as much as you do, and I am willing to sacrifice anything," Sharon said with silent tears streaming down her face.

They went to their room and got the suitcases out of their closet, packing for a month. Who knew how long they would be away? After packing, they carried their bags to Harry's car, climbed in and pulled out of the driveway, making their way to the airport.

Ten minutes and one tense car ride later, they arrived at the airport, parked and walked inside where Harry made a beeline for the long queue to buy tickets while Sharon walked over to an indoor café to get coffee. Waiting in line, she had the feeling someone was staring at the back of her head. Turning to confront it, she was met with a line of chattering people, none of whom were looking in her direction.

She turned around and ran her hand down her face. Since when was she this paranoid? She felt it again, somebody staring at her, watching her every move. She quickly whipped her head around and saw a man trying to duck out of her view. She left the queue to confront him; could this man be involved in Jamie's kidnapping? They were following her now, on top of everything else.

"Stop right there," she yelled as she grabbed his shoulder and spun him around to face her. She was met with the terrified, pale face of a teenage boy.

"Please stop! I just saw you on the news and wanted some cash for a photo," he begged. Tears started to well in his eyes in fear as Sharon regained control of herself and let go of his shoulder.

"I'm so sorry, I thought you were somebody else," she apologized. She watched the kid run away and out of the building as she bit down on her lip.

What were they doing to her? What was this case turning her into?

Chapter Thirty-One

The Admiral turned his head to the sound of his officer announcing the all-clear and walking back to their boat. He watched the officer approaching to update him.

"Sir, we only found handlers on board, no sign of any children," the officer admitted. He was met with an angry huff from the admiral and groans from his fellow officers.

"They all seem to have ingested cyanide. Most are dead, but some are still holding on, but not for much longer."

"I have called in Homeland and the CIA to search the vessel. They'll find anything there is to find," the admiral announced.

After about half an hour of silence and anxious waiting, the crew was rewarded by the sound of a helicopter bringing in Homeland and the CIA. The specialists climbed down a ladder onto the submarine and proceeded to process the scene inside and find hidden evidence.

"We will find every shred of evidence that there is to find down there, don't worry," assured the head of the CIA.

"Nothing will be missed. We will find something, anything that leads us to them," added the representative for Homeland Security.

"Ma'am, there is evidence that they were on board, but nothing indicating when and where they were taken," the CIA agent offered.

The Fleet Admiral dialed the cell number of the director of the FBI to update him and anxiously listened as his phone rang.

"We have an update," he said immediately the director answered.

"All the other men and women we found are dead, most likely poisoned themselves upon discovery. No children were on board, but there was evidence of their presence at some point. We need to keep this quiet for now or else the American people will only be discouraged."   The director responded, "I understand. I will update my agents and we will do everything in our power to prevent a leak."

"Thank you, I will keep you updated," promised the Admiral.

As the phone call ended, the director called Harper into his office to update her on the case. She walked in with a glimmer of hope in her eyes and sat down with her hands clasped, hoping for good news.

"They found a submarine. The men and women on board were all found dead or dying as a result of poisoning, and all the children were gone. I need you to keep this confidential, Harper," said the director.

"Yes, sir. Thank you for the update," replied Harper as she left his office. She took a deep breath, fully appreciating that she was about to risk her job by making this phone call, but he deserved to know.

She dialed Harry's phone number and anxiously waited for it to be answered. Although they hadn't found his son, he had the right to any information pertinent to the case, confidential or not.

"Harry, I shouldn't be telling you this but there has been an update in the case."

Chapter Thirty-Two

Jamie scanned his surroundings as the man who had brought him into the room along with other kids gently lifted him up and set him onto the surface of whatever it was that he had been traveling in. He was now certain it wasn't an airplane, Airplanes didn't float in the sea. He felt a sense of hopelessness at not recognizing what it was he was standing on.

He was shoved into the group of kids already out there when he heard the roar of an approaching motor. Could he dare assume that help was on its way? After the ordeal he had been through over the last few days, it had become hard to imagine the cavalry, so to say, coming to his rescue.

"Vamos, Vamos," a bald man with a Spanish accent commanded the children as he rushed them to the edge of the submarine.

Jamie turned around to find that the nice man gone who had brought him up the stairs, and his heart sank. He scanned his surroundings to see only anxious faces of many guards, all armed and pushing the kids towards the left side of the submarine. When he was pushed closer to the front of the group, he saw a boat idling beside the submarine.

"Vamos!" the woman on the boat angrily encouraged the men helping the children over the side rail and into the vessel.

The guards responded with a heightened sense of urgency and began lifting the children and setting them down on the deck of the boat to be herded together in the cabin below. Jamie felt himself being lifted and whimpered as he was released and then pulled down the ladder.

Although he was terrified, he couldn't help but feel relieved and even a sense of excitement. He would see his parents again! Just a few days away from them had seemed like a lifetime of separation. He felt himself starting to smile in spite of himself; he was finally going to see them again. They would know how to make him feel better; they always had.

"There's no reason to smile, they are lying," said one of the boys already onto the boat, a scowl etched into his face.

"Really?" Jamie whimpered as tears started to form in his eyes.

Taken

"We've been kidnapped, and nothing has changed. We will never see our parents again," replied the boy with pity in his eyes.

Jamie felt the tears spill over and slide down his face as he realized that the boy was probably telling the truth. Why would these people go to all this trouble just to bring them back in the end? They weren't returning him to his parents, and he was still in danger. He sighed and decided to just rest for a minute.

Jamie's eyes flew open as the guards on the boat started yelling in Spanish and frantically lifting and depositing kids. With a sharp intake of breath, he felt himself being lifted up, exhaling only when he was released and set back down. He felt a guard's hand on his back and surveyed the area on which he stood. He whipped his head towards the sound of an engine and saw a big truck approaching.

As he contemplated how far he could get or if they would use deadly force if he ran, he felt a guard grab his waist from behind. He whipped around to see that the back of the truck was now open and crying kids were being forced physically into it. He scurried into a dark corner by himself in an attempt to claim some measure of personal space.

A few minutes later, a loud slam reverberated the load body as a guard glared at them before pulling a heavy metal door down on the back of the truck. They were instantly enveloped in darkness as the truck pulled out into the street and drove away.

Only a few hours later, Jamie felt as if they had been traveling for days. They were all sweating and had become increasingly dehydrated during the uncomfortable journey. They had stopped once to allow the kids opportunity to use the bathroom. Some kids had probably lied just to get a whiff of fresh air. Maybe they even thought they would be able to summon help, which proved to be an impossible feat at that point.

Jamie tried as hard as he could to focus on the situation at hand, but it was hard when all that consumed his mind was thoughts of water. He had no idea where he was, and he seemed to have more sweat on his skin than saliva in his mouth. As he tried to formulate a useless escape plan just to pass the time, he felt himself once again succumbing to sleep, and he finally gave in.

Chapter Thirty-Three

"We've landed, honey," Sharon shook Harry's arm to wake him.

Harry slowly opened his eyes and looked around the plane, confused by the many smiling faces. How could these people be happy when so many innocent children were missing? Not only children in other countries, their own children, too. But they had dismissed it as if it was of no consequence whatsoever. As if, since they had been unable to solve the case at the time, it somehow became pointless to pursue the matter further.

He made the conscious decision to overlook his view of the situation as his wife took a hold his hand and helped him to stand up. He softly squeezed her hand as they walked down the aisle and exited the plane together. Having recovered their luggage, they saw a man carrying a sign that read, 'Harry and Sharon'. They approached him and when he spoke, they recognized his voice from their phone call.

"What I'm about to tell you is classified, but you deserve to know," Detective Ramos whispered to them. They shook their heads with serious expressions, trying their best to show him that they understood the gravity of the situation.

"We have a list of names of people that you can speak to for answers," he said as he slipped Harry a folded piece of paper.

"You will have to —" Ramos attempted before he was cut off by Harry's cell phone loudly ringing..

"This is Harper, I have to take this. I It could be an update on Jamie. I'm sorry," Harry insisted. The detective nodded in understanding as Harry accepted the call.

"Harry, we have a new theory. We think that they are taking the children back to Columbia to be sold as sex slaves or to be illegally adopted by rich families," Harper explained.

Harry's stopped breathing as he silently prayed that Jamie was being sold to a rich family so that he didn't have to consider the implications of the alternative.

"Thank you for the update. I have to go," replied Harry. After he ended the phone call, he nodded to his wife meaningfully and turned to address detective Ramos.

"That was Harper. We have to get to Columbia as soon as possible, but is it still alright if we follow up with all the people on this list?" Harry asked, holding up the folded page.

"Of course," replied Detective Ramos.

Harry turned to his wife and said, "We need to find these people and question them as soon as we can. I'll explain later, but right now we need to buy tickets to Columbia."

Jasper Joshua West

Chapter Thirty-Four

Jamie was shaken awake once again by a stone-faced guard who then jerked him into the air by his arm and then set him back on his feet. He felt the guard's hand on his back, guiding him to the edge of the truck's load body. His arms were yanked, and he was once again set down. He tried to look around in the dark, and his eyes focused on the building into which the kids were being pushed.

The armed guards on either side of the double doors were watching the children, probably to scare them just enough to stop them from trying to run. But would they really fire on them if it came down to it? Shoot innocent, scared kids who were just desperate to see their parents again?

While contemplating that, he was pushed through the doorway of the building, following the other kids into a room with the word 'Kindergarten' displayed on the door. Faced with dozens of sleeping pads spread out throughout the room, he was led towards one and pushed to sit down. Once all the kids were seated on their own mats, two guards left the room, leaving the other two on either side of the doorway, constantly scanning the room.

The guards returned, one carrying a box of juice cartons and the other peanut butter and jelly sandwiches. They moved through the room, handing each child a juice box and a sandwich. All too soon the children were all drinking and eating as if they hadn't eaten in days, which was very likely in most cases.

As time went by, most of the kids either cried themselves to sleep or fell asleep as soon as they put their heads down on their assigned mat. Jamie scanned the room and saw an older boy still awake next to him. When he saw Jamie turn his head towards him, he tried to feign sleep, but Jamie saw that his eyes were open before he did so.

"I know you're awake, you don't have to pretend," whispered Jamie.

"Alright then. My name is Dan, what is yours?"

"Jamie," he whispered sadly.

"Well, Jamie, I have no idea where we are, but I think I can find out."

"How? They aren't speaking English," asked Jamie.

"I know that, silly. I speak Spanish and I can hear them through the walls if I stay quiet enough," Dan offered by way of explanation.

"Yes! Please tell me what they are saying about us," Jamie said excitedly.

"Shhh! You'll get us caught. I must listen now," Dan said putting a finger to his lips to signal for Jamie to be quiet. He closed his eyes and they both held their breath, listening to them talk, and Dan started translating.

"We will only stay at this school for one night. Some people will come here tomorrow to look at us," Dan whispered, clearly terrified.

Jamie felt the terror on Dan's face reflected on his own as he discovered what the guards were saying about them. Who was coming to see them tomorrow? And why did they need to look at them?

Chapter Thirty-Five

Two boys pushed open a heavy door and stepped out of the room into the streets of Cartagena, Columbia, looking to the sky in wonder, as if they hadn't seen it in months. The two boys ran down the street as if their lives depended on it and came to a halt in front of a police officer.

"We are from Panama, taken by bad people. We escaped," the oldest boy frantically explained with his arm around the younger boy.

The officer looked at them dismissively and said, "Go back to your parents, this is not funny." He assumed they were just delinquents trying to prank them, and turned his back to them, signaling for them to leave.

They walked around to face him, and the younger boy said, "Please, we are in danger and we do not know where we are."

The officer seemed to register the looks of terror on their faces and took their rant more seriously. It registered that they pronounced their words differently and that they had foreign accents.

He turned to them with a serious expression and asked, "What happened to you?"

The youngest boy spoke up in response, "We were taken from the street in Panama months ago. They took us to a hotel here where bad men hurt us."

The officer took them down to the station to be held until further notice, having reported the crime.. The sergeant called him into his office a few minutes later and told him to leave the kids in the waiting room.

"The CIA caught on to this case quickly; they are on an emergency flight right now and they will be here shortly. Organize a team for a raid on the hotel immediately. This case is becoming much more public than it was ever supposed to be," the sergeant addressed the officer.

The assembled task team together with the officers arrived outside the doors of the shabby, run-down hotel identified by the boys. They formed a line on either side of the doors and the head of the team signaled for them to wait.

"This is the police. Open the door or we will have to use force," he announced with the help of a megaphone. When he was met with silence, he signaled to his team to use force to get in.

In a coordinated act, they kicked in the double doors and entered the building with their weapons drawn and at the ready. An officer found and turned on the light switch, and they were bathed in light. They searched the rooms to find meals not eaten and suitcases in the process of being packed..

The head of the team cursed, "They must have started packing when they realized the kids were missing. They were tipped off before we got here, and now they are in the wind."

He relinquished his gun in favor of the walkie talkie from his belt and said, "Question the kids and then bring them back to where they were taken from."

Harper walked out of the meeting with a grim look, disappointed with what the FBI chose to do with the intel from the raid. To 'avoid panic' they took it upon themselves to keep the entire situation classified. A fancy way to say that they were keeping it a secret from the American people because they unilaterally decided that the public wouldn't be able to handle it.

They decided on sending additional officers across the various agencies to Cartagena to assist in the search for the remaining victims. Regardless of the FBI wanting to keep it under wraps, she had to call Harry and let him know about the update.

Jasper Joshua West

Chapter Thirty-Six

Harry and Sharon walked into the police station for a last-minute check-in with Detective Ramos before leaving Panama. Their eyes met across the room, and he smiled and motioned them into his office.

"Harry, Sharon, good morning. Another case has been opened in Columbia with an uncanny resemblance to our case. I would like to share the details with you."

"What is it?" asked Sharon, sharing a hopeful look with Harry as they waited for him to explain the connection.

"Two boys were found running on the streets in Columbia, claiming to have been kidnapped from Panama. They were held in a hotel for months and managed to escape of their own volition. Unfortunately, all the kidnapped children and the kidnappers were gone by the time the local police arrived. They have questioned the boys and are currently investigating," Ramos explained.

"What did the boys have to say?" asked Harry, sounding not nearly as desperate as he felt.

"That's why I called you in here, sir. After they were kidnapped, they were taken by boat to Columbia.

As the lead investigator of the Panama abduction cases, Ramos wanted nothing more than to give the parents hope. No. That was not accurate, he noted in his own mind on reflection. What he wanted most of all was to return the child to the parents. His goal in life was to rescue the vulnerable and do all within his power to give them full opportunity to lead a normal life as a family. He did not have children of his own, after very nearly a decade of an otherwise near-perfect marriage. He and his wife, Angeli, had been more excited than either had imagined was possible when she was deemed to be with child. Their child would have been a honeymoon-baby had it survived to full term gestation. But providence had a different fate in mind for the couple. They would endure two more failed pregnancies, and then no more.

Through all those emotionally demanding years and physically taxing losses, Angeli and Bori Ramos had been uplifted by the lyrics penned so many years before by Oscar Hammerstein II.

> *"When you walk through a storm, hold your head up high, and don't be afraid of the dark. At the end of the storm, there's a golden sky, and the sweet silver song of the lark. Walk on through*

> *the wind. Walk on through the rain, though your*
> *dreams be tossed and blown.*

> *Walk on, walk on, with hope in your heart and*
> *you'll never walk alone."*

All hope would sadly be wrested from their hearts as Angeli failed to conceive for a fourth time.

It was the Ramos's misfortune to have firsthand knowledge of losing a child. Was it worse to lose a child with whom a bond was only formed in uterus, or a child who had years to form a personality while in your care as a parent? Losing a baby before 24 weeks of pregnancy requires no burial or cremation. This was the situation with the Ramos's first baby. The hospital did however offer the grieving parent a sensitive option to cremate the 18-week-old fetus of their somehow perfectly formed little girl together with the remains of other miscarried babies. The parents, clutching at straws, had seen it as their baby girl's chance to enter the afterlife with the souls of those who had 'suffered' a similar fate. The hospital chaplain had, by way of providing some form on solace, suggested that the baby had in fact not suffered at all.

"Did Christ our Lord not say: Suffer little children to come unto me and forbid them not: for of such is the kingdom of God. Verily I say unto you, whosoever shall not receive the kingdom of God as a little child shall in no wise enter therein."? Those had been his words as he committed the remains of the yet-to-have-lived to whatever it was that awaited them in what may have been eternity. Or may not have been. That was one of the hardest difficulties to face. The not knowing what was in store for their dearly departed. But they chose to hang on to the hope and the promise of paradise.

It did not get easier with each loss. They had been taken to a different hospital when Angeli showed signs of bleeding during her first trimester. Sad to say, the hospital handled the remains of this early loss as clinical waste simply because the distraught parents had not specifically requested otherwise.

The third baby, a son, had been born with a mop of black curls and a distinct cupid's bow. Angeli had delivered him days before he would have been considered typically full term after she had been to see the doctor because she had not felt movement for a day or two. The team in the delivery room, constituting a doctor, the nurses and a midwife had not attempted resuscitation given that the baby had already been dead in utero. So the little blue boy had been placed on his mother's chest, and the parents given time to say their plaintive goodbyes.

That was the end of their losses. But also the beginning of their existence as those who would never parent their own biological child. They made the decision not to follow the option or adopting. If Providence deemed them to be childless, then there had to be a valid reason and they would respect their lot in this life.

Taken

Detective Bori Ramos would make it his life's mission to ensure that those who had the privilege of being parents, would be reunited with their lost and stolen children. No one should ever feel the weight of losing a child. Not on his watch. His mission was personal and that made it non-debatable.

Chapter 36

Jamie had no idea how long he had slept, but it wasn't long. Sleep had kind of crept up on him and having slept most of the day before certainly hadn't helped. When the men woke him, he was as confused as he usually was after a short nap.

Dan had fallen silent a few hours in, but he still looked tired. Their captors had shaken them awake one by one, handing out bottles of water and ham sandwiches as a breakfast offering.

The majority of the kids in the room had been awoken earlier by the opening of doors and the unnecessarily loud men, but no one appeared to care.

The man spoke quickly, shoving those kids who had finished eating towards the back of the room.

"What's happening?" Jaime asked Dan in a hushed whisper as he was pulled ahead of him.

"It's okay," he replied, looking around to Jaime. "They just want us to take a quick shower and then we'll change into clean clothes."

Jaime scowled, but with enduring the heat, a shower and a fresh set of clothes didn't sound too bad. He was sweating constantly and smelled terrible, and so did the rest of the children around him.

Taken

It seemed odd that they had gone to the trouble of kidnapping the children and dragging them out to the middle of nowhere in the heat, just to hand out food and fresh clothing. Nevertheless, having the men shout at him in a language he didn't understand was terrifying. His first instinct was to resist them just because they were forcing him. Seeing Dan going along with what they were doing calmed him somewhat, and he found himself in a group shower similar to those at his school gym.

The cold water was a welcome shock after the all-consuming oppressive heat, and it left Jaime spluttering and shivering in its aftermath. He had no idea how he was going to make it out of here, but the shower and a fresh set of clothes was enough to calm him some.

He was still a little hungry. The sandwich hadn't been enough to fill him. His mother liked to say that a growing boy needed to eat. Her breakfasts were the best. He missed her, not only for the breakfasts, of course, but as his stomach growled loudly, that was certainly what was on his mind. Just bacon, scrambled eggs and buttered toast with jam was all he could think about as he pulled on the new clothes.

Simple clothes were provided; short-sleeved shirts, shorts, socks and shoes. Fresh clean and his exact size. He did have to admit to feeling a little better.

The children were all lined up outside, in the courtyard of the school. The men spoke as if they were expecting someone to arrive.

But after what seemed like hours of standing around during which no one arrived, the men were looking anxious and angry. They snapped at those children who tried to talk to them.

Nobody was coming and they didn't like that. Before the sun reached its peak, they were all lined up and sent back inside. Maybe they were going to be provided with lunch, too.

Chapter Thirty-Seven

Agent Harper stood outside the abandoned school while her team conducted the search. The boys who had escaped had mentioned abandoned schools in the area used to house the children. Having searched three schools, they had yet to make any form of discovery linked to the disappearances. The FBI and the CIA were working together with the Columbian police on this, and they were expecting results not limited to merely charging into the local abandoned schools.

Nothing. A few showed signs of having been lived in, maybe even in the kind of numbers that the boys had indicated, but the apparent residences were now long gone.

"They've been tipped off," Harper said as the agents came out empty handed once again. Two teams were raiding other local schools, but by the looks of it, they weren't having any luck either.

"What makes you say that?" asked Aquino, a member of the Columbian cop contingency.

"They knew that we were going to be raiding the schools," Harper replied, shaking her head. "If it was just the one that the boys escaped from, that would be understandable, but they pulled at least three places clear. That means that someone tipped them off."

"Who?" Aquino asked, shaking his head.

"Well, I don't want to insult your fellow officers around here, I know you're a local..."

Aquino tilted his head. "Where are you from?"

"Born and raised in Florida, but you're a local, right?" Harper countered. "How likely would you say it is that your fellow officers might have let the kidnappers in on our plans?"

Aquino didn't look happy about this line of questioning. His mouth opened, but after a few seconds of thought he paused and snapped it shut again.

"It's a possibility," the officer finally said with a shake of his head. "I mean, sure, corruption is a problem, and them having alerted the kidnappers is possible, but there are some things that you just don't do."

"So, there are acceptable and non-acceptable levels of corruption?" "That's not what I meant, and you know it," Aquino said. "You kind of understand the guys that take a little money on the side to let dealers get away with a bit here and there; that's business. And while it's not acceptable, the guys back at the station don't get too hot under the collar over it. You get to charges of kids being taken, that changes things, you understand?"

Harper nodded. "Well, whether or not it's a possibility for us to look into doesn't really matter. We need to find those kids, and my government has deep pockets, deeper than those of whatever gangs are paying off your officers. So, if you could spread the word around that we'll be grateful to whoever helps us, that would be great."

The officer eyed the agent closely for a few moments before sighing. "I'll see what I can do. For now, though, this place is empty. Let's get out of here."

Chapter Thirty-Eight

The lunch wasn't much more satisfying than the breakfast had been, but it was still better than nothing. More peanut butter and jam sandwiches, more water, and then they were told to take what Dan called a 'siesta'.

"It's what you call it when people take a nap in the afternoon, until it's not so hot anymore," the older boy had said as they all settled into their too-small beds and waited for any sign from the men detaining them.

"They don't let us do anything," Jaime whined as he settled into his bed, crossing his arms rebelliously across his chest. "I'm bored."

Dan shrugged his shoulders. "Maybe they think that we're going to run away. There aren't enough of them to watch us all the time, so if we're always indoors and easy to watch, nobody's running anywhere."

"Still sucks," Jaimie complained.

"Yeah, it does," Dan said, leaning back into his bed, shaking his head. "But it could be a lot worse."

"How do you mean?"

Dan didn't answer, raising his hand, moving a little closer to the door where they could hear a couple of the men with raised voices outside. Jaime still couldn't understand whatever language they were speaking, more than likely Spanish, but they sounded angry.

"What are they saying?" Jaime asked, whispering.

"They're talking too quickly," Dan replied, shaking his head and focusing intently. "They're talking about the client. No, the buyer. The buyer is late. Or they aren't coming. And he doesn't like it. They want to talk about staying longer, but they don't want to hang around here any longer."

"Why not?" Jaime asked. "I hate them just pushing us into trucks and driving us all over the place."

"People are looking for us," Dan said. "They don't want to wait around. But they don't want to lose the buyers either. He's talking about how it was difficult to get us all the way down here, and he didn't do it just for the fun of it."

"Don't think anyone's having fun here," Jaime grumbled.

"The buyers are late, so they have to move us out of here," Dan continued, still trying to discern what they were saying. "Anyone that wants to continue can contact them… they're moving us again."

Taken

The news was received rather numbly by the rest of the kids, who looked up at the door in response to elevated shouting outside. And then they all heard the sound of the truck being started up again.

"Do you think they'll find us?" Jaime asked.

"I hope so," Dan replied with a small, brave smile.

"Me too!" Jamie said, the excitement bringing a smile to his face.

Jasper Joshua West

Chapter Thirty-Nine

There was not any level of choice of places to eat out here in the middle of nowhere. The officers had nonetheless found themselves here and it wasn't likely they would be moving on to the next spot without at least trying out one of the local street-side restaurants.

Well, restaurant was a little strong, Harper found herself thinking as they arrived at an eatery of sorts place. The appearance suggested that it had been erected by hand without the necessary skills. The majority of the plastic chairs and tables were outside on the porch where patrons could have the benefit of wind and natural air movement, since there was no chance of any form of air conditioning.

The team was able to secure a few seats at the tables, ordering whatever was available that seemed likely to be hot and edible. The local officers were somewhat more trusting, ordering bean stew or chicken with rice. Harper, for her part, was going with whatever was cooked most thoroughly. She ordered a plate of empanadas with a side of the same bean and sausage stew the others were having.

She was hungry, not stupid. As much time as she spent sampling the street food in Miami, Harper doubted that her body was built for the kind of food served hereabouts.

And sure enough, she was hissing as the spicy heat started building in her mouth after only a few forkfuls.

Aquino laughed when he saw the FBI agent red in the face. "They say around here that you can't taste the food unless it's burned into your tongue."

"I actually appreciate the spices," Harper admitted. "Means that the food is preserved."

"Whatever you say, man."

The owner came over to top up their drinks, looking very cautious around the local officers. "Most of the dishes that we serve here are going to be a little hot for the people. But if you prefer, we can get you something that's a little less *caliente*, yes?"

"*Diablos, no,*" Harper said, laughing and then taking a gulp of her drink. "Hot is fine."

"Well, we have some left over from that order we took from those *coños* that came around near closing time last night when we were shutting up," the owner said with a chuckle. "The bastards asked us to cook up a whole bunch of food, and asked for it not to be too spicy, since it was for the *niños*. Who the hell waits until that late to feed their kids?"

Harper blinked a few times before looking up at the man, narrowing her eyes. "Wait, did you deliver to these guys?"

"*Si,* they didn't have the time to wait for us to prepare the food," the owner said. "Gave us directions to a school down the road about fifteen miles and then up the dirt road down to the left."

Harper was almost loathed to believe what she was hearing, looking back to their list of schools in the area. None that the owner had mentioned were in the location.

"Damn it," Harper said, turning to her men. 'Mount up, and fast. There's a school nearby to check. Now, damn it, now!"

The owner looked afraid as they began to rush out while Harper pulled out a few bills to more than cover their orders.

"Thanks for your help, my friend," Harper said, pressing the bills into the man's hand.

"*De nada?*" the owner replied questioningly, but Harper was already headed to a car.

Jasper Joshua West

Chapter Forty

There were a few places in the world where Harry had never supposed he would end up, even on vacation. North Korea was at the top of the list, but northern South America had always been fairly high too.

Horror stories about what the local drug lords were capable of doing to tourists had always ensured neither he nor his family would ever be found anywhere nearby.

Yet here they were. Finding a small hotel in which to stay just seemed so inconsequential compared with finding their son. In the absence of anything else to do, they weren't going to just stand around waiting for something to happen.

They secured phones that would allow them to stay in touch, but the local law enforcement told them that all they could do was wait by the phone for their call.

Harry wasn't sure why he was surprised to see his phone vibrating almost across the extent of the bedside table.

He pounced on the device before Sharon could, answering it and pressing it to his ear.

"Mr. Giles?" came Harper's familiar voice. Before Harry could reply, she continued, "Just thought that you should know that there has been some intelligence on your son. Children have been reported as being held in a school near to Cartagena. I'll text you the location."

Harry looked down at his phone after Harper had hung up, to see the details of the location she had texted.

"That's not far from here," Sharon said after consulting her laptop. "We can be there in less than half an hour."

Neither thought that it was a good idea to be near a police operation, but they didn't have much of a choice. They got to their rental car and followed the directions which Harry had downloaded on his phone.

They arrived a few minutes after the officers had concluded their sweep . It seemed to have been recently cleared. A pile of dirty clothes had been left behind on the makeshift beds that had been set up for the kids.

"Who are you?" a local officer asked, walking over to the pair. "You cannot be here!"

"That's fine, Aquino, I'll handle them," another responded in perfect English. "Mr. and Mrs. Giles, I presume? We found a few documents that might interest you."

In his extended hand was something which Harry couldn't quite make out in the moment. As his vision cleared, he realized what he was looking at.

"That's my Jaime!" Sharon said loudly. "That's his school ID! Did you find that here?"

The man nodded. "They only left a couple of hours ago, at the most. They couldn't have gotten far, not with the roadblocks that have been set up."

The two returned to their car. They weren't sure what they were going to do but going back to the hotel seemed implausible. They weren't ten minutes down the road before they hit a roadblock.

But it didn't appear to be stopping too many people, who merely detoured, taking advantage of the available side roads.

"What are you doing?" Sharon asked as Harry made to follow suit.

"The roadblock isn't stopping anyone," he replied, not looking back at her. "Let's see where the people that know this place might be heading?"

Chapter Forty-One

Jamie had learned not to resist the men when they were in a hurry. A couple of the kids had, but they were yelled into submission, cooperating while crying.

The kids were rounded up in a hurry and loaded back into the truck, and it wasn't long before they were on the move yet again.

They started out fast but slowed down abruptly as if they might be caught in traffic. The heat beat down on them mercilessly, crowded into the covered load-body. Jaime could feel sweat soak through his shirt when they finally came to a halt, and a hurried conversation was heard outside.

"Police," Dan whispered to him.

"Can they help us?" Jaime asked, suddenly filled with hope.

Taken

That feeling quickly dissipated as he turned back to his friend and saw his dejected look. The conversation outside was a lot less tense than Jaime expected it to be, and after a few minutes they started moving again.

They were moving faster now, and after a minute or so had passed, they were suddenly on a very bumpy road. The driver didn't bother slowing down and hitting the more severe bumps at high speed had caused the kids inside o be tossed around like shuttlecocks.

Jaime was holding on, trying to keep from being thrown off his feet. A couple weren't so lucky, and they were falling about and hitting their heads.

Those who gave in to crying, though, were quickly stopped. One of the men shouted at them, sounding angry and unlikely to be tolerating any more noise from the group. Jaime could see a couple of them reaching for weapons, but none were drawn.

It felt like hours had passed, but it was less than thirty minutes before they stopped again.

Jaime could feel more than a few bruises swelling up from being knocked against the sides of the truck. The men had quickly dismounted, resulting in more conversation between them.

"What are they saying?" Jaime whispered to Dan.

He shrugged. "I can't hear them."

It was pretty faint, but again, they appeared to be talking with a person they knew with whom they were going to be doing business.

The tone of voice was the same as the one Jaime's father used when he was talking to a business associate. Kind of fake, and yet the effort that was put into faking it made it sound real.

They didn't talk for long, and finally the truck started moving again after only a few minutes. The road was still bumpy, but the going was slower this time.

Once they came to a halt, the men started shouting and indicating for the children to move off. Jaime looked around, seeing that they were in what looked like an old barn.

"Where are we?" he asked, still whispering.

"Somewhere that the police won't find us," Dan said, looking like he was struggling with maintaining his impossible optimism.

Taken

Chapter Forty-Two

"What are you watching?" Harry asked, stepping out of the shower.

Sharon looked around at him. "Oh, they're talking about a police operation in a hotel on the other side of Cartagena. They found a group of kidnapped kids being held there and arrested a group of the kidnappers."

"Wait, what?" Harry asked. "Since when do you speak Spanish?"

"Since never, I got a call from Harper while you were in the shower," Sharon said, her voice in a low monotone.

He didn't need to question her mood. He'd seen this coping mechanism in the past.

"I guess... Jaime..."

"He wasn't with the kids they recovered," Sharon said, her voice trembling slightly. "I... well, it's nice, since quite a few parents are now reunited with their children."

Harry tried to smile, but it was a struggle. Sure, he could be happy for the families that had been and would still be reunited, but their Jaime was still missing and out there, somewhere, all alone and scared.

"They're going to find him, sweetie," Harry said, hugging his wife closely. She hugged him back, and a few seconds later he could feel her sobbing into his chest. "They're going to find him."

Chapter Forty-Three

The longer they stayed in that damn barn, the tenser the situation appeared between the men who were their captors. Not one appeared to be willing to leave, but it wasn't long before they showed signs of needing more than just the shelter that that barn provided.

Food and water became an issue between the men during the two days that they were to spend in the barn until they were finally willing to move again. Jaime couldn't remember being this hungry ever in the past, but he moved with the rest of the kids, trying to keep his spirits up.

It was difficult, but not impossible.

Back in the truck, they only moved at night until they reached what looked like a small compound buried deep in the nearby mountains.

An abundance of food and water was available here, and they were all treated to a welcome hot meal, followed shortly after by showers and another change of clothes. Those that they had worn during their extended time inside the barn had quickly become ragged.

The group of men looked a little calmer and a lot more relaxed. It was a relief to have sufficient food and water supplies, but the children were still restless, unsure as to what would be happening next.

Once they were finished dressing in their new clothes, they could hear a car pulling up near the building that served as their makeshift prison. Jaime craned his neck to see a tall, dark-skinned man coming over and talking to their captors, shaking their hands and patting them on the side of the head, in a way that made it seem that he was comforting them.

It took him a few minutes to find his way to their group, smiling broadly and showing a perfect set of pure white teeth.

"Good evening, children, how are you all tonight?" he asked in perfect English.

There was no response. Jaime had no idea just how they were expected to respond in this situation.

"Alright then," the man continued as if he hadn't been expecting an answer anyway. "My name is Sam, and I'm here to make sure that you're all very, very comfortable. Things might seem a little confusing now, but don't you worry about a thing. It won't be long before you all get set up with your new families. Families who will love you very much. You might miss your mommies and daddies now, but soon you'll be rich, and forget all about them, okay? Now get some sleep."

Sam turned and walked away, and the guards guided them towards the beds that they would be spending the night in.

"At least we have real beds this time," Dan said, settling into the cot next to Jaime's.

Jaime didn't answer, curling up on the clean sheets as the lights went out. He didn't know what they were talking about. He didn't want a new family, rich or otherwise. He wanted his own.

He couldn't help the few tears that escaped his eyes, running slowly down his cheeks to drop onto his pillow. More came. Sobs wracked his chest even as he could feel himself drifting off, dreaming of home.

Taken

Dear Reader,

Thank you for reading Grounded! I hope you enjoyed the story. **I've included a <u>FREE BOOK</u> below and a sample of another book on the next page**.

It would be awesome if you could let others know what you thought of my book by leaving a review on Amazon!

Thanks again,

JJW

Get your FREE copy of Escaped:

bookHip.com/lkcwpk

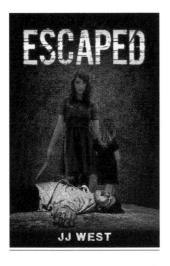

Or type in **bookHip.com/lkcwpk**

Having trouble? Just email me. I'll add you to my list and send you a copy! jjwestauthor@gmail.com

Jasper Joshua West

Keep reading for a free sample of:

Grounded

http://bit.ly/GroundedVig

Chapter 1

Day 1: Sunday

Dennis Coleman woke up first. Light was already streaming in around the curtains. He looked at Sarah, who was sleeping peacefully on her side of the bed, her light brown hair covering her face. He watched her sleeping for a moment, then he turned and picked up his smartphone from the bedside table and checked the time. 7:56. Normally the kids were up at sunrise and they woke him and Sarah up not long after, so there was no need for an alarm clock on the weekends. To add to his good mood, there were no new emails waiting for him this morning, probably for the first time in months. It looked like it was going to be a good Sunday.

Dennis used the bathroom, stood in the hallway listening to the quiet for a moment, then headed back into the bedroom. He was still a little sleepy, and he was also hoping that he and Sarah could make love before heading downstairs. He nuzzled up against her and planted a kiss on her cheek. She moaned but did not stir.

He closed his eyes but instead of drifting off, his mind wandered to his messages. He had certainly sent out enough yesterday, and because of the time difference, his clients in Asia usually replied while he was sleeping. Perhaps they had all decided to take Sunday off for once and he would hear from them in the evening.

As if in answer to his thoughts, his phone chimed with an incoming message. He snatched it up to find it wasn't an email but a text message. The number was blocked and the message read: "YOU ARE ALL GROUNDED!" Dennis instantly dismissed it as some sort of spam, and he was about to put the phone back on the table when he noticed there was no cell signal. He must have just lost the signal as it had to have been working for the text to come in.

The Wi-Fi icon was also missing from the status bar on his phone, which was strange because he always kept his phone connected, even while he was sleeping. Opening the menu, he determined that the phone's wireless adaptor was turned on but couldn't detect any wireless networks in range. Dennis scowled as he considered the money he had spent setting up three Wi-Fi access points in the house.

Even if the one on the second floor wasn't working, he should still be able to get a weak signal from the one downstairs.

Normally the internet going down in the house wouldn't have been a big deal, but with no cell signal, his mobile data wouldn't be working either, which meant his clients had no way of getting in touch with him. He was a very successful man, a leader in his field, but that could change really fast if he was unavailable when his clients needed him. There was, after all, plenty of competition in the business.

Dennis sighed again, put on a bathrobe, and went to have a look at the Wi-Fi router which was mounted on the ceiling in the hallway. The power light was glowing steadily, but all of the other lights were dark. He wasn't exactly sure what all of those little lights were supposed to indicate, but the fact that they were all off was not a good sign, he was sure. He had glanced at the router before and normally there were several lights glowing, some of them steadily and some of them flashing randomly. He assumed there must either be something wrong with the router or there was no internet signal coming in. Dennis didn't know what to do besides turning it off and turning it back on again.

On the other side of the router, he found a couple of wires going in and a button that said PWR under it. He pressed the button once to turn it off, then again to turn it back on. Then he looked at the lights on the front of the unit again. All of the lights came on momentarily, then they all went off except for the one that had been on before and the DSL light which began flashing on and off at even intervals. Dennis checked his phone again and found that he still had no Wi-Fi signal. He decided to go check downstairs where there was an identical router mounted high on the wall behind the sofa.

Dennis stood on the couch to get a closer look at the lights and found only the power light was on. He reached for the power button hidden on top of the unit and pushed it, causing the power light to go off. He then pushed it again, causing all of the lights to glow momentarily before they all went out except for the PWR light. As had been the case upstairs, the DSL light began flashing slowly on and off. He checked his phone again to find that there was still no cell signal or Wi-Fi network available.

Dennis decided it was unlikely that both routers had stopped working overnight and that the problem must be the internet line coming into the house. He found the phone number for the internet company on his phone and hit send before remembering that his cell signal was also down.

Annoyed, Dennis headed back upstairs to his office where there was a landline. He'd insisted on getting one when they first moved in. Though he had only used it a few times in the four years they'd been living in the house, every now and then a situation arose where something other than a cell phone was required. As he reached the top of the stairs and headed for his office, a feeling of dread struck him. He stopped and opened the text message again, reading the cryptic missive:

YOU ARE ALL GROUNDED!

He tried to dismiss it from his mind but this time it wouldn't budge. The message alone was not enough to concern him, but he was having trouble being okay with the internet and cell signals not working, and also the fact that everyone was still sleeping long after they usually got up. He turned away from his office and went toward the kids' bedrooms.

Chapter 2

At five years old, Mary still slept with her bedroom door ajar and a nightlight on. Dennis pushed her door open a bit more and stood in the doorway looking at the bed. It was dark in the bedroom compared to the hallway and it took a moment for his eyes to adjust. He didn't realize he had been holding his breath until he finally was able to detect the rise and fall of his daughter's chest, at which point Dennis resumed his own breathing. There seemed to be nothing out of the ordinary here except for the fact that Mary was still sleeping instead of chattering away at anyone who would listen like she usually did from dusk till dawn.

Sam was three years older than Mary. Not only was his door closed but there was a "No Trespassing" sign on the door, which was a polite way of saying "Stay out of my room, Mary, you little pest!" Dennis quietly opened the door far enough to see in. Sam didn't open his eyes but turned so that he was facing away from the light. A moment later, Dennis could hear the rhythmic breathing of his son sleeping.

Taken

Dennis quietly closed the door and, satisfied that the kids were okay, decided the next thing to do would be to try the landline. On the way to the office, he checked his cell phone again. Still no connection to a cellular network or a Wi-Fi network. As he approached the office, he scowled, suddenly sure that the office phone wouldn't work either. He walked faster, almost running until he stood over his desk, breathing hard. He stood looking at the phone for a moment; his feeling of needing to know now replaced by dread at what he feared he would learn.

As his breathing began to slow, Dennis snatched up the receiver and, as he had suspected, the line was dead. No dial tone, no error message, nothing. He pressed the disconnect button a few times and then punched a few buttons, knowing all the while that his actions were futile but needing to try them anyway.

Dennis returned to his own bedroom and was about to wake Sarah when he noticed the blue flashing light on her phone indicating a new message was waiting. Under normal circumstances, he wouldn't violate her privacy, but today he only hesitated briefly before picking up the phone and activating the display.

He intended only to check what type of message had come in; if she was getting email then there might be no reason for concern. But when he saw the icon indicating she had received a text message, as well as another icon indicating that she was not connected to the network, he immediately unlocked the screen and opened the message. As he had feared, the message also read:

YOU ARE ALL GROUNDED!

Chapter 3

Dennis wasn't panicking yet, but his heart was beating faster than usual. When he shook Sarah awake, she sensed his fear right away.

"Dennis, what's wrong?" she asked.

Having to verbalize his fears made them seem foolish and he didn't know what to say, so he handed her the phone instead. She squinted at the screen, scrunched up her face a little, and then said, "I don't get it. What's wrong?"

"I don't know, but the phones aren't working, the internet is down, and we both got the same weird message. And everyone is still sleeping," Dennis said.

"Everyone *was* still sleeping. What time is it?" she said, laying her head back on the pillow and looking at her phone again to answer her own question. She closed her eyes momentarily while Dennis looked at her intently, then she sat back up a few seconds later. "You got the same message? Kids are still sleeping?"

Dennis nodded. Sarah put her arms around his neck and pulled him in for a kiss, the message momentarily forgotten. He put his hands under her nightshirt and slowly lifted it up. They broke their embrace long enough for him to pull it over her head then began kissing again with renewed energy. She grabbed the waistband of his shorts.

They heard a bathroom door slam, meaning at least one of the children was awake. So much for a little privacy. They gave each other a knowing look then continued kissing, but she didn't pull his shorts down and they both knew the moment was over. They heard the flush of a toilet and a moment later there was a knock on the bedroom door. Dennis went to the door while Sarah pulled her nightshirt back on.

A pajama-clad Sam was outside the door, holding his own iPhone. "Dad, there's no Wi-Fi," he complained. Then, without waiting for a reply, "I'm hungry."

"Let's fix the second problem first," Dennis said, ruffling Sam's already messy hair and heading for the kitchen. "Why don't you wake your sister?"

"Wake her up? Let her sleep! We could all use the quiet!" Sam said with a smirk.

Dennis opened his mouth to scold him, then closed it again and smiled. Sam was only repeating what he and Sarah said on an almost daily basis. Besides, it was Sunday; the girl could sleep in a bit if she wanted, and Dennis himself wouldn't mind getting a cup of coffee before the chatter started.

Dennis went to the kitchen to put the coffee on and Sam went to the living room to try the TV. Of course, it wouldn't work with the internet down, but it would take him a minute or two to figure that out, so Dennis let him go. By the time he started the coffee maker, Sarah had joined him and was taking eggs and ham out of the fridge. Dennis sliced some bread and put two slices in the toaster before slicing more.

Sam appeared in the doorway. "Dad, the TV—"

"Doesn't work because the internet is down," Dennis finished for him. "You could try reading something instead. Or you could butter the toast."

Sam sat down at the table to twiddle his thumbs instead. "But Dad, I'm bored!"

"You've been awake for five minutes!" Dennis replied, a little annoyed. "Go and see if your sister's awake."

Sam mumbled, "But Dad..." but he only looked at his father for a moment before he walked out of the room, sighing audibly.

A few minutes later he came back downstairs, stuck his head in the kitchen, and announced, "She's asleep." Then he vanished into the living room.

"Den," Sarah said.

"Yeah, hon," Dennis said, looking up from slicing some tomato.

She looked worried. "What do you think the message means?"

"Nothing. It's a prank or spam of some sort," he said, trying to sound unconcerned.

"Maybe, but it's got me spooked," she said. "Does the phone in your office work?"

"Nope. No communication with the outside world is possible. Let's try to enjoy it."

"That's too many coincidences for me. Let's check on the neighbors after we eat and see if they have the same problem," Sarah said before she headed upstairs to wake Mary.

See in Store (Amazon USA): bit.ly/GroundedVig

More by JJ West

USA: bit.ly/JasperWestBooks

INTERNATIONAL: bit.ly/JasperWestWorld

Manufactured by Amazon.ca
Bolton, ON